HE WAS VERY SMALL, VERY BRAVE, AND VERY MUCH ALIVE!

William picked up the box and opened it. In a soft bed of tissue paper lay the Silver Knight. He carried a shield, and his right hand was raised with a clenched fist. After studying him for a moment, William picked him up.

To his amazement, the figure felt soft and wrinkled and warm. And it moved. William screamed and dropped it.

He watched as the small man rolled slowly over onto his side and pushed himself into a sitting position.

"What have you done with Alastor?" he called out, his voice a tiny croak.

"Who's Alastor?" William whispered.

The knight snatched his dagger from his belt and pointed it at William.

"Are you friend or foe?" the knight shouted. "I am not frightened by your size, my good sir, and I will fight you with every ounce of strength left in me, if that be your wish!"

THE CASTLE IN THE ATTIC

"The adventure William encounters in the fantasy world is intense, and his face-off with the wizard is satisfyingly dramatic."

—*Booklist*

"Winthrop has the real gift for fantasy, creating a believable imaginary world that nevertheless relates to the real world. William's attic castle is also the castle of William himself."

—Madeleine L'Engle

Bantam Skylark Books of related interest
Ask you bookseller for the books you have missed

BE A PERFECT PERSON IN JUST THREE DAYS
by Stephen Manes

CASTLE IN THE ATTIC
by Elizabeth Winthrop

THE CHOCOLATE TOUCH
by Patrick Skene Catling

CHRISTOPHER
by Richard M. Koff

ENCYCLOPEDIA BROWN AND THE CASE OF THE TREASURE HUNT
by Donald J. Sobol

GHOST IN MY SOUP
by Judi Miller

THE GREAT SCHOOL LUNCH REBELLION
by David Greenberg

THE INCREDIBLE JOURNEY
by Sheila Burnford

LIZARD MUSIC
by D. Manus Pinkwater

THE MUMMY, THE WILL, AND THE CRYPT
by John Bellairs

NUTTY CAN'T MISS
by Dean Hughes

THE PICOLINIS
by Anne Graham Estern

SNOWSHOE TREK TO OTTER RIVER
by David Budbill

THE SPELL OF THE SORCERER'S SKULL
by John Bellairs

TOP SECRET
by John Reynolds Gardiner

THE CASTLE
IN THE ATTIC

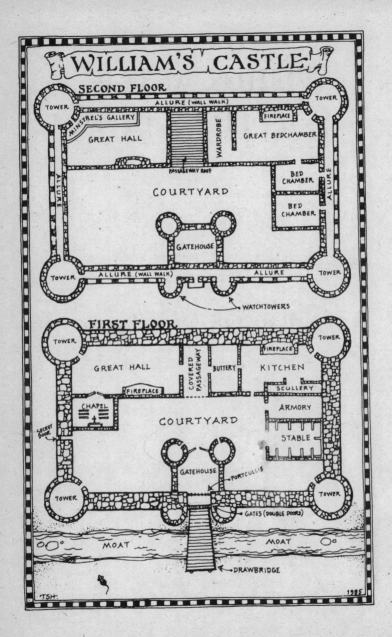

THE CASTLE
IN THE ATTIC

Elizabeth Winthrop

Frontispiece and chapter title decorations by
TRINA SCHART HYMAN

A BANTAM SKYLARK BOOK®
NEW YORK · TORONTO · LONDON · SYDNEY · AUCKLAND

RL 5, 008–012

This edition contains the complete text
of the original hardcover edition.
NOT ONE WORD HAS BEEN OMITTED.

THE CASTLE IN THE ATTIC

A Bantam Book / published by arrangement with
Holiday House, Inc.

PRINTING HISTORY

Holiday House edition published September 1985
Bantam Skylark edition / September 1986
12 printings through November 1989

Skylark Books is a registered trademark of Bantam Books
Registered in U.S. Patent and Trademark Office and elsewhere.

The author would like to thank the following two publishers for granting permission
for the two quotes reprinted in the author's note:

E.P. Dutton, Inc., for Gates of Excellence by Katherine Paterson, copyright © 1981
by Katherine Paterson. Reprinted by permission of E.P. Dutton, Inc.

Viking Penguin, Inc., for the Preface to Gone: A Thread of Stories by Rumer
Godden. Copyright © 1968 by Rumer Godden. Reprinted by permission of Viking
Penguin, Inc.

ISBN 0-533-15601-2

Published simultaneously in the United States and Canada

PRINTED IN THE UNITED STATES OF AMERICA
O 18 17 16 15 14 13 12

For ANDREW,

who has dared to cross the drawbridge

THE CASTLE
IN THE ATTIC

CHAPTER 1

On Monday afternoon, Mrs. Phillips was waiting for William at the kitchen door. He came in shaking like a dog and blowing the raindrops off the tip of his nose.

"I still can't do it," he said.

She looked disappointed. "What do you mean?"

"He's added an Arabian dive roll at the end of my floor routine. Before I even get through the hand-springs, my legs feel like jelly."

"I'll just have to help you practice some more." She turned back to the sink. "Lots of work to do. We don't have that much more time."

"The meet is still six weeks away," he said as he hung his dripping poncho on the hook by the door.

"Sit down, William," she said. "There's something I have to tell you."

Her voice was formal, distant. He sat on the stool and wiped off his face with the towel she handed him.

"I'm going to be leaving the end of this month."

"For vacation?"

"No," she said. "For good. I'm moving back to England to live with my brother."

"Why?" he asked.

"It might seem silly to you, but I'm homesick. Even after all these years. And you're getting old enough to take care of yourself."

Mrs. Phillips had been with William's family since he was born. Ten years. "I thought you were going to stay until I grew up," he said, still turning the idea around in his mind. He couldn't seem to absorb it.

She sat down at the table across from him. "Look at me."

He shook his head. If he looked at her, he might start crying.

"William, you're ten years old. You can take care of yourself now."

"How do you know?" he shouted. He shoved his chair away from the table. "You're not going to leave me. I won't let you." He ran out of the room before she could say anything else.

Mrs. Phillips owned two things that she really cared about. One was the picture of her husband, who'd been killed in World War II, and the other was her mother's pearl circle pin. When she went home to her little apartment in town on weekends, she left these two objects at William's house, where she thought they'd be safer.

"When I die, William," she often said, "be sure they bury me with my picture and my pin."

On Saturday morning, William took them and hid them in the shoebox that held his rock collection. He knew Mrs. Phillips would never leave without them.

She must have noticed they were gone right away because the first thing she always did on Monday morning was open her top bureau drawer and take them out. When she picked him up from gymnastics practice in the afternoon, she looked at him for a long time without saying anything. He got all ready to lie, but she didn't bring up the subject. On Tuesday, his father and Mrs. Phillips stopped talking the moment he walked into the kitchen.

"Hello," William said brightly.

Mrs. Phillips turned away without a word.

"Hello, William. Finished your homework?" his father asked as he drifted out of the room.

His mother was the first one to come out and ask him directly. She was tucking him into bed Wednesday night when she brought it up. "Have you seen Mrs. Phillips's picture? You know, the one of her husband that's always on her bureau? It's missing."

"No," said William. He pulled his bear up over his face.

"Well, will you please keep an eye out for it? She's also missing a pearl pin that was left to her in her mother's will. Maybe the man who came to fix the furnace last week took it." His mother rambled on, but William wasn't listening. Why didn't Mrs. Phillips come and ask him herself?

"I wish she weren't leaving," William said in the middle of one of his mother's sentences. "How come she has to go?"

"She misses England, William. That's where her brother lives. When you get older, I guess you want to go back to your family."

"But we're her family, aren't we?" William asked.

"As close as we can be, William, without sharing the blood," his mother said. "She's been with us for ten years. That's a long time." She leaned over and hugged him. "Good night. I'll see you in the morning."

"Mom?" he called as she started out of the room. "She won't leave without her picture, will she? She told me she wanted to be buried with it."

His mother stopped and thought for a minute. "She's made up her mind to go, William. I think she'd even leave her picture behind if she had to."

* * *

On Friday afternoon, when William got home from school, he tiptoed into Mrs. Phillips's room and put the picture and the pin back on her bureau. When he turned around, she was standing in the doorway. Neither one of them spoke for a long time.

"I thought it would make you stay," he said at last.

"That's what I thought you thought," she said, putting out her arms. William went and buried his nose in her newly washed dress. He cried a little. She pushed the dark hair off his forehead, swaying back and forth as she hugged him.

William held back his tears with his parents, with the boys at school, even with Jason, his best friend, but never with her. "You have a gentle heart," she once told him, as if that were a good enough reason for a ten-year-old boy to cry.

He pulled away and blew his nose with the linen handkerchief she handed him from her pocket. "I'm not giving up. I'll think of something else to keep you here," he said.

"Good," she answered, laughing. "I like my men to fight over me. But I've got a few weapons of my own. When you come home from school on Monday, I'll have a surprise for you."

"What kind of a surprise?" he asked.

"A big one," she said. "And I'm not going to say one more word about it."

CHAPTER 2

William burst through the back door on Monday afternoon. "Did you bring the surprise?" he asked. He dropped his book bag on the table and began to pace back and forth.

"You look like a horse at the starting gate," she said with a laugh. "Of course I did. It's in the attic." William turned to run up the back stairs, but she stopped him. "Wait. I want to be with you when you first see it."

"All right," he said. "But hurry up. I've been thinking about it all day."

Mrs. Phillips went ahead of him. When they reached the second floor, she stopped in front of the door to the attic. "Now close your eyes and I'll lead you up. It was too big a thing to wrap."

He put his hand into her large wrinkled one and

allowed himself to be led up the last few steps like a baby.

At the top she squeezed his hand and let it go. "You may look now, William," she whispered.

"You brought it," he cried, gazing down on the enormous stone and wooden castle she had told him about ever since he was little.

"It's yours, William. I'm giving it to you."

"Forever?" he whispered.

"Yes. It's my goodbye present."

"Then I don't want it." He sat down on the top step with his back to her and the castle.

"Even if you don't take it, I will be leaving, William. I hope I don't have to drag it back to England with me. It belongs here with you now."

"Why?" William asked without turning around.

"I haven't been reading you *King Arthur and the Knights of the Round Table* all these years for nothing." She poked him in the arm, but he didn't answer. "It's more than that. I know that you are the right person for it. You have the kind of gentle soul that accepts the rules of chivalry. If you hadn't turned out the way you did, William, I would never have entrusted the castle to you. I wouldn't give it to just anybody." Her voice seemed to get smaller, as if the words were having a hard time finding their way out, and he wondered

if she was going to cry. What did she mean by all that
stuff about a gentle soul? She seemed to think he was
special or something. He didn't like it that he cried
too easily and was smaller than the other kids in his
class, if that's what she meant by "gentle."

"All right, show it to me," he said.

"We'll start at the drawbridge," she explained, moving around to one side of the castle wall. "Got to do
this thing properly." Down on their hands and knees,
with their heads close together, they first inspected the
defenses of the castle. "You pull this lever to lower
the drawbridge," she said, reaching down inside the
front tower of the gatehouse. "Then this chain raises
the portcullis, that metal grating just beyond the double
wooden doors."

"I know what a portcullis is," William said.

"I'll take away the wooden bar that holds the doors
while you work the chain."

William reached inside and pulled, the links of the
chain rubbing back and forth between his thumb and
index finger. The metal grille disappeared into the wall
above.

"Good, we are inside," Mrs. Phillips said. "I'll give
you the grand tour."

With their eyes and fingers, they walked through the
lower floor first, opening wooden doors and peering
into the round tower rooms of the gatehouse, then

across the open courtyard to the stable. If he put his head right inside the courtyard, William could see into the empty stalls.

"This is the armory," Mrs. Phillips explained as she pulled open the small door beyond. "The weapons are kept here." Shields, lances, and swords were attached to the walls.

"The kitchen doors slide back. To the left is the buttery, where food and drink are kept cold, and to the right is the scullery where the dishes are washed up. That door in the corner opens to the tower stairs that lead up to the master chambers."

"The kitchen has a fireplace," William said, pleased.

"All the main rooms do. Look at the great hall." She slid open the door across the courtyard. On either side of the fireplace, the walls of the large banquet hall were draped with cloth tapestries. Up above, William could just see the minstrels' gallery, where troubadours and jesters sang to entertain the lords and ladies dining below.

"Feel those round circles of metal around the corner?" Mrs. Phillips said.

He nodded.

"If you pull on those, the door to the chapel will open. You can see it from this side through the stained-glass window."

He pulled and, like magic, the door opened. He ran

his finger across the cold stone floor.

"Now for the second floor," she said. "Both of the rear towers have staircases that lead to the upper chambers and also on the left and right to the wall walk. These two roof sections lift off," she said, picking them up to reveal the upper-story rooms. "On this side you see the minstrels' gallery and then down into the great hall. The other side is the master bedchamber."

"What's this little room?" William asked, poking his finger into a small space next to the bedchamber.

"That's the wardrobe, where the clothes are kept. The two rooms over the armory and stable are smaller bedrooms for servants or children. You enter them through the master chamber or through the door from the allure, which is the correct name for the wall walk. And that's the end of the official tour."

William crawled all the way around the castle. He hooked one finger into an arrow loop, blew the dust off the staircases, fastened all the doors. At last, he sat back on his heels. "It's wonderful," he said. "It's an even better surprise than I thought it would be."

"I knew you'd like it."

"Are there any knights?"

"Just one," Mrs. Phillips said, pulling a small box out of the pocket of her sweater and handing it over. "Save him for later."

"Why?" he asked.

"It's a family tradition. You're supposed to meet the Silver Knight on your own. My father made me do it that way," she explained with a shrug. "You know me, I love rituals."

"All right." He put the box down in the middle of the courtyard, even though he wanted very much to open it. But he supposed she was right. For now the castle was enough. He wanted her to know how much he liked it. "The castle's really wonderful," he said again.

She looked pleased. "Time to start dinner. It's just the two of us tonight. Your mother has a school board meeting, and your father went to look at a site."

"Where did the castle come from? Tell me again," William said at dinner.

When they ate alone, they always sat in the kitchen. The checkered curtains, the yeasty smell of Mrs. Phillips's toast spread with Marmite, and the circle of light that the green shaded lamp cast around them made William feel cozy in the big, creaky house.

She did not settle into her seat until everything was in place on the table; their plates, the salt and pepper, honey for her tea, ketchup for his noodles, and chocolate syrup for his milk.

"I hate to get up in the middle of a meal," she said.

"You say that every night."

"And I mean it every night." She poured some honey into her tea. The floating spirals of gold slipped underneath the surface, one little circle after another. "Now about the castle. Every family has its own traditions that reach back into that family's history, into another time. Other people pass on Bibles or journals or old wedding dresses. My family has always passed on the castle. It goes back as far as my father's great-grandfather and probably to before that, although we don't have certain proof of it." She took a bite and chewed on it thoughtfully. "You remember when I went back to England last year?"

William nodded, his mouth full.

"I found the castle in my parents' house when my brother Richard and I were clearing it out. That's when I had it shipped to America."

"All the way from Stow-on-the-Wold, England?" said William. He used any excuse to roll that funny name around on his tongue.

"Now all the way to Riveredge Lane, Southbrook, New York, care of William Edward Lawrence, complete with drawbridge, chapel, armory, minstrels' gallery, and one Silver Knight. The tapioca pudding is in the icebox. None for me tonight."

He cleared the table and rinsed the plates. "What about the Silver Knight?" he asked, his voice raised over the running water. "Has he always been in the castle?"

"As far as I know. I think there might have been other soldiers originally because my great-grandfather mentioned some in a letter about the castle, but I've never seen them. When I was a child, there was only the Silver Knight. There was some legend that was passed down about him. I remember bits and pieces of it. He was thrown out of his kingdom long ago by an enemy of some sort, and it's said that one day he'll come back to life and return to reclaim his land. But the whole time I played with the castle, he was as stiff and cold as lead."

William sat down again. He made paths in his pudding with his spoon before taking the first bite. He wasn't really listening to her story. The question of her leaving hung between them. It took up as much room at the table as he did.

"Afterward," he started, his voice almost choking on the word, "will I have dinner alone on a night like this?"

"Oh, William," she said quietly. When he looked up, he saw tears in her eyes. "Of course not. Don't you see, if I go now, your mother and father will spend more time with you. You and I, we're almost too close. It leaves other people out."

"The castle doesn't make any difference," said William, getting up. "I'm still going to figure out a way to make you stay."

Mrs. Phillips didn't say anything. He went upstairs to do his homework.

CHAPTER 3

William lay in bed for a long time without sleeping. He heard the front door close gently.

"That's Mom. One more to go," he whispered to Bear, who lay beside him, dressed in William's old sweatshirt.

William's mother was a pediatrician. She had evening office hours so that working parents could bring their children in for checkups. "So who takes me to checkups?" William once asked.

"Mrs. Phillips," his mother replied. "That's why I'm able to work. I know you're in good hands."

William didn't answer because he knew that was true. But something about it gnawed at him.

Last year, his mother had run for the school board, so now she had meetings after office hours twice a month. But that was all right, too, because Mrs. Phillips was always there on weeknights.

William listened to the sounds his mother made as she moved through the house. "Let's pretend we're asleep," he whispered to Bear. He lay still as she pulled the blankets up to his shoulder and tucked them under his chin. She leaned over and kissed him on the right temple. The smell of her perfume hung in the air after she'd left.

The headlights of the second car swept across the ceiling as Dad pulled into the driveway. "Number two," William mumbled into the pillow. More doors and running water and some whispering in the hall, and then the big house was quiet.

He let a little more time go by, just to be on the safe side, and then got very quietly out of bed. "Come on, Bear, let's go upstairs and get that knight out of his box." He pulled his reading flashlight out of the drawer in his bedside table and crept down the hall with Bear tucked securely under his arm.

William knew just how far to open the attic door so that it wouldn't creak. He and Bear slipped through without a sound. He flipped on the light switch and left his flashlight on the bottom step. The castle loomed above him, a great gray shadow. He was glad he had brought Bear.

"All right, your lordship, I have come to meet you," William announced in a loud voice in order to cheer himself on. There was an odd, expectant feeling in the attic.

He propped Bear up against an old trunk and knelt down. In the middle of the courtyard the small box sat right where William had left it. He picked it up and opened it. In a soft bed of crumpled tissue paper lay the Silver Knight. He carried a shield decorated with a cross in one corner and the small carved figure of a lion in the other. William noticed the sword was missing from the knight's scabbard, although his dagger was in place on his right hip. His right hand was raised with a clenched fist, as if he were challenging some unseen enemy. After studying him for a moment, William picked him up.

To his amazement, the figure felt soft and wrinkled and warm. And it moved. William screamed and dropped it. With a tiny clanking noise, the knight fell back down into the courtyard.

William grabbed Bear and pounded down the stairs. He stopped outside the attic door. "He couldn't really be alive. I must have imagined it," he said as he tightened his hold on Bear. He opened the door again and peered up the stairs. There was no sound. "Come on," he said. "I'm not going to be scared by a lead

knight that's two inches high." With that pronounce-
ment, he marched back up the stairs and peered over
the wall of the castle.

The knight was still lying on the ground where William had dropped him. William gave him a little push
with his finger. The man's tiny arm fell across his
chest. *He really is alive,* William thought.

"Are you all right?" he asked.

He watched as the small man rolled slowly over on
to his side and pushed himself up into a sitting position.
He pulled the metal helmet off his head and set it down
carefully beside him, smoothing the red plume with
his fingers. At last, he looked up a very great distance
to William. When he opened his mouth to speak,
William leaned down to listen.

He asked a question in what must have been his
normal voice, but William couldn't understand him.

"Say it again, a little louder, please," William called.

The man covered his ears with his hands.

"Sorry, I didn't mean to shout," William said more
quietly. "You talk louder and I'll talk softer, okay?"

The knight tried again. "What have you done with
Alastor?" he called out, his voice a tiny croak in the
courtyard.

"Who's Alastor?" William whispered.

The knight struggled to get up, but his legs wouldn't

work properly. Still sitting, he snatched his dagger from his belt and pointed it at William. William had to work hard to keep from laughing at the ridiculous position the knight was in.

"Are you friend or foe?" the knight shouted. "I am not frightened by your size, my good sir, and I will fight you with every ounce of strength left in me, if that be your wish."

William stifled a giggle. He was being threatened by a seated miniature man waving a pin-sized knife!

"It might be easier to fight me standing up, my lord, although I don't doubt your strength or courage. Let me help you up. I am your friend and shall ever remain so, if you will allow it." William was quite proud of his little speech. Those hours of reading about King Arthur with Mrs. Phillips had paid off after all.

The knight put away his dagger, and slowly William placed his index finger down close to the man's shield. He leaned on William's extended finger and pulled himself to his feet. The knight did not let go immediately, so William held himself very still, the way he had once when Jason's parakeet had landed on his outstretched palm. At last, the small man felt steady enough to support himself, and William drew his hand away. *He is as tall as my index finger,* William thought to himself as he sat back on his heels.

Both were quiet as the knight adjusted the sleeves of his tunic and gave his metal shinguards a quick shine with his handkerchief. His motions were precise and unhurried. Using the wall for support, he moved his legs about slowly, bending and unbending them at the knee. Then he worked out the kinks in his arms.

"You look like me when I'm warming up for gymnastics," William said. The knight didn't answer. Although William was bursting with questions, he waited for this small person, who was clearly used to making people wait, to finish pulling himself together.

"I thank you for your patience, kind sir," said the knight. "Allow me to present myself. I am Sir Simon of Hargrave, known in my own country as the Silver Knight."

"I am glad to meet you," William replied, remembering his manners. "I am William Edward Lawrence. I'm sorry I dropped you. I thought you were made of lead, and then when you moved, I got scared. I felt a little prick. It must have been your dagger."

"May I ask, is this country peopled entirely by giants?"

William grinned at the question. He'd certainly never thought of himself as a giant. "Yes," he said. "I am one of the smaller ones."

"And are they all friendly?"

"Not always," William said thoughtfully. He wasn't sure either of his parents would be happy about this tiny intruder living in their attic. "But you're safe," he added. "The only ones who ever come up here are me and Mrs. Phillips."

"And who, may I inquire, is Mrs. Phillips?"

"She's the one who gave me the castle. She played with you when she was small. But I don't think you ever came alive for her. At least, I'm sure you were made of lead this afternoon. What happened?"

"You must have broken Alastor's spell," Sir Simon explained. "But wait. Where is the magic token? I snatched it from Alastor just before he spoke the words. Where has it gone? I must find it." The little man, looking desperate, got stiffly down on his hands and knees and began to search the floor.

"What's it look like?" William asked.

"Like a medal with the face of a man on one side."

William leaned over the courtyard. "It probably dropped out of your hand when you fell. You start over there, and we'll meet in the middle."

They both searched in silence for a while, William running his finger back and forth across the courtyard as if he were spreading glue on the floor. Suddenly, he hit something that skidded across the space toward the knight. They both went for it, but William got there first, and he picked up the tiny round piece of metal. With a demanding air, the knight stepped back and thrust out his hand.

"I just want to look at it for a minute," William said, ignoring Sir Simon's impatient gesture. It was about the size of a baby aspirin, and on one side he could just make out the outlines of a man's head with two raised lines next to it. Tiny hinges stuck out from either edge at the level of the man's ears. William flipped it over. The other surface was smooth and empty. "It's hard for me to see it clearly," William said. "I wish I'd brought my magnifying glass."

Sir Simon took it off the end of William's out-stretched finger and put it carefully away in a pouch that hung from his belt.

"Why's it so important?" William asked.

"I believe we were talking about Alastor's spell," Sir Simon said. "You are the one who broke it, and I am exceedingly grateful to you."

"Why was I the one who broke it?" William asked.

"It must have something to do with who you are," Sir Simon said.

"But why me?"

"I don't know, and I don't intend to find out tonight. If you would be so kind as to direct me to the bed-chamber, I will take my leave."

William had more questions, but he decided they could wait.

"Of course, my lord, this way, please." With his forefinger, William slid open the door to the kitchen. "On the far side, you'll see the stairs leading up to the bedchambers. I'll leave some food for you in the kitchen tomorrow morning, but I can't stay to talk then. I'll come up again for a visit in the afternoon."

"Till we meet again," said the knight. After a slight bow, he disappeared through the kitchen door. *He is the perfect size for the castle*, William thought.

"Too bad you slept through all that, Bear," William whispered as he found his way back down the stairs. "It would have been nice if someone else had seen it happen. Then I'd be sure it wasn't just a dream."

William fell asleep with his thumb rubbing the small pinprick the dagger had made in his palm.

CHAPTER 4

Mrs. Phillips liked to sleep late in the mornings and brew her tea using the electric kettle in her bedroom, so William always ate breakfast with his parents.

"What are you doing in science now, William?" his father asked.

"We just started using microscopes. It's boring because Mrs. Phillips and I have been doing it for ages. Right now we're looking at frog's eggs."

"What about history?" said his mother as she stirred her coffee. "Still on the Spanish settlers?"

"Nope. The Southwest Indians. I have to write a paper on how to build an adobe house."

"Maybe your father could help you. He spent some time in Arizona."

"I was only fifteen at the time, Anne," his father said. "And those were the days when I wanted to be a movie star, so I didn't pay much attention to the local architecture." He winked at William.

William pushed his soggy cereal around in the bowl. He had to get the spotlight off himself so he could scrounge some food for the Silver Knight. "How's your work, Dad?"

"Jim Harrison and I walked over the site for their new house yesterday. It should be an exciting project because of the topography of the land."

"Really?" his mother asked. "I would have thought that land behind the school was very flat."

While they talked about the Harrisons' house, William slid a piece of toast and half a slice of bacon into his napkin and tucked them up his shirt-sleeve.

"May I be excused?" he asked. "I promised Jason I'd meet him early to go over some homework." William's face grew red the way it always did when he tried to lie, but his parents were too busy talking to notice. Anyway, Jason usually got to school early, so William had only told half a lie.

"Certainly, dear," his mother said with a vague smile. "Be careful riding home on your bike this afternoon." She said the same thing every day.

"See you tonight," said William as he headed up the stairs.

* * *

"Sir Simon?" William called softly. "I've brought your breakfast."

There was no answer. He waited for a minute, half expecting to hear the clank of the small man's metal shoes on the stone staircase.

"I'll leave it for you in the kitchen. See you later."

William crumbled up the bacon and half the toast and piled it on the kitchen table.

"Maybe I did dream the whole thing," he muttered to himself as he wheeled his bike out of the garage.

Jason was waiting for him in the front hall. He and Jason had been best friends ever since first grade. William was the shortest kid in the class and Jason wore thick glasses, so they were usually the brunt of everybody's jokes. Hanging out together had helped them develop tough skins and deaf ears.

They walked up to the classroom. As usual, they had it to themselves for a few minutes. Nobody else in their class ever got to school early.

"You're late today."

"My parents were asking me the usual questions. How's school? How's science? How's history? How's life?"

"You're lucky," Jason said. "My parents never ask me anything."

"That's because your mother is home when you get there in the afternoon. She doesn't think she has to concentrate on you the way my mother does."

"Yes, she does. She just concentrates on the wrong things. Like, have I practiced the piano and did I put out the garbage? That's why I spend half my life over at your house. Listen, did Mrs. Phillips change her mind about leaving yet?" Jason asked.

"No," William said. "But she brought the present she promised me."

"I forgot all about that. What was it?"

"A castle," William said.

"A castle?"

William nodded. "It's got four towers and a complete gatehouse and a chapel and a roof that lifts right off so you can see inside the bedrooms on the second floor."

"Can I come over this afternoon and see it?"

William didn't say anything for a moment. He hadn't decided yet whether or not to tell Jason about the Silver Knight. The other kids were filing into the classroom.

"Find your seats, please," the teacher said as he closed the door behind him.

"Can I?" Jason whispered.

"Not today, okay? I have to go to a special gymnastics practice," William lied. "Maybe tomorrow."

The day seemed to drag by. The Silver Knight stayed in the back of William's mind all afternoon, and the teacher had to remind him twice to pay attention. By the time he left school, he had convinced himself that his adventures the night before were just a dream.

"You're home early," Mrs. Phillips said. She was down on her knees by the flagstone walk in the front yard.

"What are you doing?" William asked.

"Turning over the soil for the border annuals. If the weather stays this warm, I'll be able to get the plants in before I leave." She started to get up.

"I don't need a snack today," he said quickly. "You can finish what you're doing."

"But I thought we had to practice the back handsprings. I was going to spot you today."

"I want to play with the castle for a while. I'll be down soon."

"All right," she said. She went back to her digging, and he stopped at the kitchen door to glance at her. The curve of her back, the way her white hair fell down across her cheek, her crisscrossed gardening shoes tucked neatly under her skirt . . . Everything about her made him feel safe and happy.

He grabbed an apple from the bowl on the kitchen table and went up to the attic, turning over and discarding his various plans for making her change her mind about leaving. None of them seemed right. He knew he had to do something soon. He was so distracted by these thoughts that he almost tripped over the castle.

"Young man, hold up, hold up," cried the Silver Knight, who was standing on the wall walk, waving frantically at William's knee.

"Sorry," William said, dropping down beside him. "I was thinking about something. I didn't see you."

Sir Simon looked indignant at the thought that anybody could forget about him. "In your world, sir, I may be small, but in my own, I am known as a man to be reckoned with."

"I'm sure of that, Sir Simon," William replied quickly. Working his penknife out of his front pocket, he chopped a slice of apple into tiny chunks and put them down on the battlements of the wall. It didn't seem proper to put a knight's food on the floor. "I brought you something to eat," he said. "I'll bring you more after dinner."

Sir Simon ate quickly, spearing each piece of apple with his dagger. William lowered the drawbridge, and the knight joined him at the top of the attic stairs, glancing cautiously about him as he scrambled across the wide planks of the floor. William lifted him carefully up onto a trunk that had been pushed against the wall.

"To defend yourself against any unseen enemy, you should always keep a wall at your back," Sir Simon remarked as he settled into a comfortable sitting position.

"If you don't mind, sir, I want to know where you came from and how you got here," William said.

"I thought you would have some questions when you returned, young man. I cannot answer them all."

"Can you tell me what you do know, then?" William asked.

"Certainly. I hope you are comfortable because this tale will take me some little while to tell."

William nodded. "Please start."

"Very well, then. I was the only son of my father, Lord Aquila, a noble and powerful knight who was, at the end of his life, a very sick man. He contracted an unknown disease that caused his limbs to weaken and shake so that, for days at a time, he would take to his bed. We called in respected doctors from all over the land and even from across the ocean. They did no good, although they charged high fees. It cost us dearly to board their servants and stable their horses while they took their time considering the matter of the disease and conferring with one another."

At this point, the knight, clearly upset, got to his feet and began pacing back and forth. William was worried that he might fall off the edge of his lookout. But after a while, he grew calmer and sat down again.

"At that time," Sir Simon went on, "there was a

wizard in my father's kingdom by the name of Alastor.
Some months before my father grew ill, this man had
arrived at the castle one morning, seeking employment,
and my father had taken pity on him. He was a raggle-
taggle sort when he first appeared. His robe was torn
and dusty, and he talked of having traveled long dis-
tances and having suffered much. From the beginning,
I was more suspicious of his story than my father and
pressed Alastor for details. He gave none.

"At first, Alastor seemed perfectly harmless. He
was given a room down near the kitchen where he
sometimes invited me to help him mix up potions and
salves that were supposed to straighten crooked bones
and settle upset stomachs. He had a wardrobe in the
room that he always kept locked, and I noticed he was
careful never to open it when I was there.

"The more I saw of Alastor, the less I really knew
him. He was a man of secrets, some of which he told
me, but more often I heard tales of the wrongs that
had been done him. The stories were garbled and I
didn't pay much attention to the details, but I sensed
even then his desperate need to control people, to have
power. Let me give you an example.

"Around his neck, the wizard wore a length of woven
ribbon from which dangled three medals or tokens.
Once, early on in our acquaintance, when he still trusted
me, he pulled that necklace out of his robe and showed

it to me. In the middle hung a small, flat disk made out of lead. At the time, I did not find it particularly interesting. I know better now. Hanging from the ribbon, on either side of the disk, there were two halves of one medal that showed the two faces of Janus. They had hinges, and Alastor told me that they could be fitted together when necessary but he preferred to use them separately."

"The word January comes from Janus, doesn't it?" William asked.

"Precisely," Sir Simon said. "I see your education has not been entirely neglected. Janus guards the gates of heaven and looks both ways in time. But the image of Janus on Alastor's necklace had an evil, magical power. One half of the token made things small, and the other restored them to their normal size. The symbols beside Janus' head on each surface were different. The side that made things small showed two staffs, the instruments of punishment. The other side showed two keys.

"I saw him work this magic on a rat. When he pointed the staff side, the rat shrank to the size of a toy. When he used the side with the keys, the rat returned to normal. I am convinced that most of Alastor's magic lay in that necklace, but I never learned much more about it because after a while he grew secretive around me.

"Meanwhile, my father got steadily worse. The doctors were totally mystified. I suppose I was the one who thought of asking Alastor for help, though now I curse myself for the idea. He came and sat by my father's bed, asking about the symptoms and making a long list in some strange language. The next day, the wizard began administering an evil-smelling potion to my father, who took it reluctantly, as the taste was as bad as the odor. To our amazement, he appeared to get better. The palsy seemed less violent, and my father had long periods of peace when he could rest.

"It was not until much later that I realized the drug that helped him sleep was also slowly poisoning him. Alastor was hailed as a genius by all of us, and my father insisted that the wizard be given a large bedroom right next to his own. To everybody's relief, the doctors were bundled off to wherever they had come from.

"My father became quieter with every passing day, and he slept a great deal. When he was awake, he insisted that Alastor stay near him, for he felt the wizard was responsible for his recovery. I often came in to find them deep in conversation, and my father began to grow suspicious of me and of his own trusted councillors. Alastor was poisoning his mind and his body at the same time."

William's legs were beginning to ache, so he shifted position.

"I am taking too long to tell this story," Sir Simon said quickly. "I will hurry. Just days before my father died, he issued various edicts through Alastor. In these, the councillors were sent on missions to neighboring kingdoms. They objected, knowing my father was near death. It meant that they would have to return to the kingdom through the forest. Alastor had put some sort of spell on the forest to protect our kingdom from attack, and we knew the councillors would not be able to get back through. We were convinced Alastor controlled my father's every action, but my father would not even see us to listen to our arguments. Alastor had moved his pallet into my father's room, and he even ate his meals there. The councillors had no choice but to leave, and after that, my only friend in the castle was my old nurse, Calendar, who had been with me since birth. She and I sat up late into the night discussing plans for defeating Alastor, but they came to nothing.

"My father died at last, and if there is anything I can thank Alastor for, it is that he went peacefully and without pain. But I can never forgive Alastor for turning my father against me. At the end he would not speak to me at all, saying that I had been a traitor to him and to our kingdom." Sir Simon stopped speaking and covered his face for a moment.

Then he went on. "The day after the funeral, Alastor

came to my room and showed me a paper that my father had signed before he died. It proclaimed that Alastor was to succeed my father as I was not fit to rule. Calendar was with me at the time. I was dressed in a full suit of armor, as I was about to review the guard. I ripped the paper to shreds, and the two of us attacked the wizard. Alastor pulled the necklace from under his robe, pointed the lead disk at me, and mumbled a word. I reached up and snatched at the necklace, which fell off his neck. One half of the Janus medal came away in my hand. He lunged at me and tried to get it back, but I curled my fingers around it and held on. Calendar was trying to pull him off me, but I could not help her because by that time, Alastor's spell had begun to work. The bottom half of me had already turned to lead. I could not move my feet or bend my knees."

The knight shuddered, remembering that moment. "It was horrible. I cried out to Calendar but she was no longer struggling with the wizard. They were both watching me, he with a terrible smile on his face, and Calendar . . ." The knight stopped speaking for a moment as if he were trying to work out something in his mind. "I realize now that Calendar deserted me in the end. It was too late to save me, and she must have known she would be left behind with the wizard. At the very last moment, as my face was growing smooth and cold, Alastor flipped the lead disk and pointed the other side at me. Then everything went black. And the next thing I saw was you."

"So the other side of the lead disk made you small?" William asked.

"No, it must have sent me here. I am not small in my own country, young man, only in yours." The Silver Knight patted the pouch that hung from his belt. "This is the weapon that makes things small, the token I stole from Alastor."

"How do you know it still works?"

"Why, I had not thought of that," said the Silver Knight, pulling apart the drawstrings of his pouch. "I suppose we had better test it out on something."

William glanced around him. "Here, try this," he said, placing an old pincushion on the ledge in front of the knight.

Sir Simon extended both arms, and, holding the token before him like a shield, he pointed it directly at the pincushion. Nothing happened.

"I remember Alastor muttered something when he used it on the rat," the knight said.

"Try the word 'small,'" William suggested.

"Small," said Sir Simon.

The pincushion remained the same. They tried five or six other words, but still nothing happened.

"Perhaps it only works on living things," Sir Simon said. He glanced up at William thoughtfully.

"Oh, no, you don't," William said, standing up. "You can't try it on me because you couldn't make me big again. There'd be nobody to bring you food, and you'd be in terrible trouble when Mrs. Phillips came looking for me."

"It was only an idea, my dear sir. Do not alarm yourself," Sir Simon said. "But how else will we know if it works?"

"I know, I'll bring you a bug or something tomorrow."

Suddenly, the attic door opened down below. "William," Mrs. Phillips said. "I've been calling you. It's dinnertime."

William reached down and scooped up Sir Simon so that the knight was safely hidden in his hand by the time Mrs. Phillips started up the stairs. "I'm coming," he said quickly. Mrs. Phillips stopped at the tone in his voice and gazed up at him.

"Everything all right?" she asked.

"Yes, just fine," he said as casually as he could. "I'll be there in a minute." He could feel Sir Simon squirming inside his hand, so he loosened his hold enough to give the little man some air.

"All right, then," she said as she headed back down

the stairs. "Don't forget, you've still got your home-work to do, and we haven't practiced the back hand-springs in two days."

"That was close," William said as he set Sir Simon on the wall walk. The knight was gasping for air, and some minutes went by before he was able to speak.

"My dear sir, more gently, if you please. I am no longer made of lead."

"Sorry, it had to be quick," William explained. "Listen, if you ever hear the attic door open and I knock three times on the wall, that means you must hide quickly because somebody is with me."

The knight nodded.

"See you later when I bring up your dinner."

"Until then," Sir Simon said weakly.

"I'll catch a bug tomorrow," William added as he went down the stairs.

CHAPTER 5

William managed to sneak an entire miniature meal upstairs after dinner. He didn't hang around to talk with the knight because he still had history homework to do. He left Sir Simon digging enthusiastically into his bits of ham and baked potato. William had even found a top from an empty vanilla bottle and filled it with milk for the knight to drink.

The next day Jason bugged him again about the castle.

"Come on, William. After all the stuff you've told me about it, I want to see it," Jason complained.

"All right, you can come home and see it today, but you have to go to gymnastics practice with me first," William said.

"I thought you had a practice yesterday."

William looked away. "We have a big meet next month. The coach is really pushing us."

"Sure, I'll come," Jason said. "It's more fun than practicing the piano."

The other members of the team were already on the floor warming up when they arrived.

"Hey, Lawrence, you're late." Robert, the coach, never let them get away with anything.

"Sorry. Can my friend watch if he stays out of the way?"

"Sure. We're starting with floor work today. After you warm up, I want to see a round-off and then two back handsprings."

"Are you going to spot me?"

"The first time. Then you're going to try it on your own. We still have to add the Arabian dive roll. The meet is exactly one month from today."

Despite all the time and energy it took, William loved gymnastics. It was the only part of his life where having a small, wiry body really paid off. His moves were faster and more graceful than anyone else's, which improved the team's scores at the meets. But it also meant Robert was tougher on him.

"Stay here, William. I want you to try it again. The rest of the group can start work on the parallel bars."

Robert walked across the room and put both hands on William's shoulders. "Remember, the back hand-springs create the momentum and speed that you need for the dive roll. Focus on your shoulders. They will do the job of transferring the energy from your arms to the rest of your body."

William plodded wearily back to the corner. This was the fifth time in a row. His arms and shoulders ached. He stopped in the corner and closed his eyes for a moment. Nobody spoke. He made himself forget about Jason waiting in the corner, about the Silver Knight waiting in the castle, about Robert's frown. He had to get the rhythm, the push, the sense of space from inside himself. One step and he started off with a powerful run, then did the round-off, and two tight handsprings. It was better, he knew that.

Robert nodded. "Join the rest of the group at the bars now."

"He really pushes you," Jason said on the way home. "Doesn't it get to you?"

William nodded. "Sometimes. But he's a good coach. And he's usually right."

"The first four looked okay to me," Jason said.

"I was crooked. I could feel it, and any judge would see it. Just like when you miss a note on the piano."

Jason nodded.

* * *

"You boys look tired," Mrs. Phillips said as they collapsed into the kitchen chairs. "Bad day at school?"

"Robert made me do the first part of my routine five times in a row," William said. "Let's not talk about it."

Mrs. Phillips put out another cup of juice and two cookies for Jason. When she turned back to the sink, William slipped a cookie into his napkin. Jason saw him but didn't say anything.

"I'll be in the front, turning over the other half of the flower bed," Mrs. Phillips said. "What are you boys up to?"

"William's going to show me the castle," Jason offered. "Is it true you gave it to him to keep forever?"

Mrs. Phillips glanced over at William. "Forever," she said. "If he wants it that long."

"Come on, Jason," William muttered.

"I bet she's sad she's leaving," Jason said as they went up the back stairs.

"She's not that sad or she wouldn't go," William said.

"I bet—"

"I don't want to talk about her, Jason."

"Okay, okay, sorry."

They dumped their backpacks in William's room and

headed down the hall. "What's the cookie for?" Jason asked.

"What cookie?"

"The one you hid in your pocket."

"Oh, that." William opened the attic door. "I leave one up in the castle for a snack. Sometimes I sneak up here after bedtime." He banged on the wall three times.

"Why are you doing that?" Jason asked.

"The light doesn't always go on at once. Banging the wall seems to help," he said as he flipped the switch. "What's with all these questions?"

But Jason didn't answer. He had vaulted up the top three steps ahead of William and was already staring at the castle.

"I never thought it would be so big," he said as he walked all the way around it. "Show me how the drawbridge works."

William moved slowly to pull the lever, giving the Silver Knight as much time as possible to hide. He thought he saw something moving in the stable, but Jason didn't seem to notice. "You pull this chain here to raise the metal grating," he said.

Jason tried it a couple of times. William sat back and let him explore the castle on his own. He was hoping Jason would finish quickly so that he could get on with his bug search, but Jason was settling in for the afternoon.

"Where are all the soldiers?" he asked.

"It didn't come with any," William lied.

"A castle isn't much fun without knights. Maybe we could pool our money and buy some."

"Sure," William said, but he knew he didn't sound very enthusiastic. He didn't want Jason around every afternoon, or he wouldn't have any time alone with the Silver Knight. He stood up. "We'd better go down now. I've got a lot of homework to do."

"Aw, come on, I just got here," Jason said. They looked at each other. "You act as if you really don't want me around."

William didn't answer for a moment. He wanted to explain everything, but he couldn't tell about the Silver Knight and he was tired of lying. "It sounds stupid," he said at last. "But I just want to be alone."

"All right," Jason said as he started down the stairs. "I guess I understand. 'Bye, William."

" 'Bye."

He knew Jason was hurt. *It's all Mrs. Phillips's fault*, he thought. *I wouldn't feel this way if she hadn't decided to leave*. He stood up.

"You can come out now," William called to Sir Simon as he rummaged around in a trunk for a small cardboard box.

Something moved behind the stable door, and the small knight appeared. "You didn't give me much warning," he shouted up at William.

"Sorry," William said. "I didn't know Jason would run up the stairs so fast. I've got to go now. It'll be dark soon, and I want to find a bug so we can test the token. I found a cardboard box to keep it in."

"I hate to trouble you further, William, but might you have something to eat?"

"Oh, I almost forgot. I brought you a cookie," William said, digging down into his pocket. "It's mostly crumbs now, but that makes it perfect for you. Be back later," he called from the bottom of the steps.

"Jason left quickly," Mrs. Phillips said as he joined her in the flower bed.

"He had to go home," William said. "Have you seen any bugs around here? I need one for my science class."

She handed him the trowel. "Help yourself. All sorts of things are feeling the spring and stirring around."

It was a warm afternoon for April. They worked side by side in silence. William found two sow bugs and put them in the cardboard box with some dirt and a couple of leaves. Then he worked on the flower bed with her.

"Have you been playing with the Silver Knight?"

she asked after a long silence.

He didn't lift his head or answer for a minute. He hadn't thought yet whether he should tell her about Sir Simon.

"Yes," he said. "He told me a very long story yesterday about where he came from."

Mrs. Phillips smiled. "Did he, now? He never talked to me all those years I played with him. There was that legend about him. Maybe it's the same one the Silver Knight told you."

William shrugged. "Maybe," he said. She wasn't taking him seriously.

"Oh, there's that gray cat from next door," she said. "Chase it away, will you, William? Every time it gets close I start to sneeze."

By the time he got back she had gathered up the gardening tools and gone inside. They said no more about the Silver Knight.

CHAPTER 6

It was past nine. William had finished his homework and his supper. Once he had said good night to his parents and Mrs. Phillips, he crept upstairs to the attic with the two bugs, his flashlight, and his magnifying glass. He wanted to take a closer look at the token.

The knight was waiting for him. The round circle of the flashlight found him in the middle of the courtyard.

"Could you bring up a candle next time you come? I have preparations to make, and I find it difficult to work when there is no moon."

William smiled. "I can leave a small lamp on all night if that would give you enough light. Nobody will notice it from the outside because the nearest house is hidden by a row of trees."

The Silver Knight watched from the lowered draw-bridge as William connected two extension cords and dragged an old bedside lamp over to the castle. "We don't use candles anymore, Sir Simon. Somebody discovered electricity about a hundred years ago. If we flip this," William pushed the light switch, "a light goes on."

"A miracle," said the knight, his eyes blinking in the sudden brightness.

"I brought two bugs and my magnifying glass. Oh, and this," William said, producing a small plastic con-tainer filled with cut-up food of various sorts. "None of this will go bad, so you can eat whenever you want instead of always having to wait for me."

William put his hand through the doors of the kitchen and propped the container on its side against the back wall of the room. That way the knight wouldn't have to climb into it to reach his dinner. Sir Simon picked through the small bits of dried fruits, granola, cracker crumbs, and crumbled potato chips. He scooped a selection of foods onto his plate.

"Could you please move this wooden table to the courtyard?" Sir Simon asked. "I have always fancied eating in the open air, and it would mean you and I could talk while I dine."

The knight stood out of the way in the corner of the

kitchen as William arranged the table and two benches in the middle of the courtyard. Sir Simon settled down to eat.

"I do not mean to be critical, my lord, but I do long for a good slice of venison and a tankard of dark ale."

"We have deer in the woods, Sir Simon, but I don't think I'd be too good at shooting them," William said with a smile. "While you're eating, could I see the token again? I'd like to take a closer look at it under my magnifying glass."

The little knight produced the token from his pouch and handed it over. Holding the medallion carefully in his palm, William moved close to the light to look at it. The head of Janus was clearly carved in the metal, and the leer on his face looked evil under the magnifying glass. William handed it back. "Was Janus smiling on the other side of the token?" he asked as he got out his box of bugs.

"I doubt he was smiling, but, as I recall, the expression was a friendly one," Sir Simon said, making room on the table.

William lifted the top of the box and peered in at the two bugs. "Well, they're still alive," he announced. "Are you ready? They're quite big. If they come out of the box quickly, they might knock you over."

Sir Simon looked mildly alarmed.

"What word are you going to use this time?" William asked.

"'Janus,'" said Sir Simon. "It seems the obvious one."

He stood at the ready with the token held out in front of him. William tipped the gray creatures out onto the table. They moved away sluggishly at first, unused to their new freedom. William glanced at the knight. When he looked back at the table, the sow bugs were gone.

"What happened?" he cried. The knight pointed at the floor where two specks of black pepper seemed to be moving about by the table legs.

"They reached the edge of the table just as I said 'Janus,'" Sir Simon exclaimed. "We have found the word that makes the token work!" He walked over and speared both beetles cleanly with his dagger before William could stop him.

"Why did you do that?" William cried.

The knight popped them in his mouth and chewed thoughtfully. "Not bad. A little dry but tasty." He wagged his finger at William. "They would never have survived this world at their size anyway. You are too squeamish for your own good, young William. And now, if you will help me clear away the food, I shall return to my training exercises," the knight announced.

"The armory is well equipped in this castle. I have found quite an adequate sword to replace the one I left behind."

"What are you training for?" William asked as he put the table back in the kitchen.

"For my return," Sir Simon said. "I shall be going back to reclaim my kingdom from Alastor."

He seemed so sure of himself that William was reluctant to tell him it was impossible.

"How do you plan to get back there?" he asked quietly.

"It will happen when everything is in place. There is a riddle written over the front door of the castle, young William," the knight explained. "You would do well to read it."

William lay down on the floor so that his eyes were level with the arched double doors of the entrance. Peering through his magnifying glass, he read the words with the lamp tipped toward them.

> *When the lady doth ply her needle*
> *And the lord his sword doth test,*
> *Then the squire shall cross the drawbridge*
> *And the time will be right for a quest.*

"But who is the lady and who is the squire?"

The knight shrugged. "We shall find out in due course. Until then, I shall prepare myself."

"Is it okay if I watch?" William asked.

The knight didn't reply. He stood in the stableyard, his sword at the ready, advancing on an imaginary target. With a roar, he made a thrust, first to the left and then to the right, ducking and weaving all the time to avoid the blows of his adversary. William watched in silence. He could see that the knight was quite agile and a powerful swordsman. *But what good would that do against Alastor's magic powers?* William wondered.

At the bottom of the attic steps, the door opened and the overhead light went on suddenly. Sir Simon ran for his hiding place in the stable. William froze. The face that appeared at the top of the steps was his father's.

"It's ten-thirty, William," his father said. "I thought you went to bed hours ago."

"I couldn't sleep, so I came to play with the castle," William said, getting up.

His father looked around. "I haven't been in the attic in years," he said. "I suppose we should clean this place out sometime. It's a terrible fire hazard."

"You say that every year, Dad," William said, edging toward the steps. But his father didn't get the hint.

"It's quite a remarkable castle, isn't it?" he said. "I had to help Mrs. Phillips carry it upstairs on Monday morning. She told me she was giving it to you to keep."

"That's right," William said.

"Show me how it works," his father said, getting down on his hands and knees.

William showed him the drawbridge and the portcullis and then took him on a tour of the bedroom wing, staying as far away as possible from the stable. But his father wanted to see it all. "What's over on this side?" he asked, poking open the kitchen door.

"That's the kitchen," William said.

"Look at that fireplace. It even has a roasting spit."

"It does?" William hadn't noticed that before.

His father's eyes wandered toward the knight's hiding place.

"That's just the stable, Dad," William said loudly. "Nothing in there to see."

"Why, look, there's something lying here on the floor," said his father, picking up the Silver Knight's shield. He handed it to William. "Some brave soldier on the run must have dropped it."

Before William could answer, there was a sound downstairs.

"William, are you up there?" It was his mother's voice. He groaned. This was turning into a party.

"We're coming down," his father called quickly.

"Be right there." He grinned at William. "We've got to raise the drawbridge and lower the portcullis. Can't leave the castle defenseless." William nodded. He hadn't seen his father this excited about something in a long time. "You realize this castle is missing a very important part of its defenses?"

"It is?" William asked.

"The moat. It needs a moat. I'll make one out of wood in the workshop. I'll come up next week and measure for it."

"Great, Dad," William said. He wasn't going to get his hopes up. His father had lots of enthusiasm at the beginning of projects, but somehow they never got finished. "I guess we'd better go down." He put the thumbnail-sized shield back on the table in the great hall.

His father leaned over and turned off the small lamp. "Guess we don't need this anymore."

William hesitated. "I like to leave it on," he said. "Just in case."

His father looked at him. "In case of what?"

"Oh, nothing," William said as he started down the stairs. "I was just kidding."

CHAPTER 7

The image of the token nibbled around the edges of William's mind for a couple of days. He kept thinking about it. On Friday afternoon when he went up to the attic, he found Sir Simon had zapped a mouse with it. The knight was standing over the small dead body, cleaning the blade of his dagger.

"Where did he come from?" William asked.

"I think he smelled the food in the kitchen. I must say it does look like the kind of thing a mouse would eat," Sir Simon said scornfully. "Anyway, I cornered him in the great hall and pointed the token at him from a safe position behind the door of the chapel. Could you bring me a fire stick from your hearth when you next come?"

"What for?" William asked suspiciously.

"I prefer my meat roasted, although I will eat the mouse raw if need be."

"I don't see why you have to eat him at all," William said grumpily.

"I must keep my strength up."

"All right, I'll get some matches for you if you promise to get him ready while I'm gone."

When William returned with a box of matches, a small quantity of wood shavings from the fireplace box, and some other supplies, the knight had cleaned and skinned the mouse. William struck a match and lit the small fire in the kitchen.

"I wouldn't have to keep a fire going all night if I had those magic sticks," Sir Simon said. "But since I cannot strike them myself, I will use the wood to keep my fire fueled through the night."

"I've brought you this too in case of sparks," William said as he put down a small mustard jar filled with water and a toothpaste cap for scooping it out. "Please be careful, Sir Simon. My father would be furious if he knew there was a fire going in the attic."

The knight nodded absent-mindedly, and William left him humming cheerily as he turned the spit.

It was almost the end of April. Mrs. Phillips would be leaving in a week. William asked her to come and watch his gymnastics practice because she would be gone before the big meet.

"Are you still worried about the floor exercise?" Mrs. Phillips asked as they were waiting for the bus.

"Yes. I haven't gotten it right yet. Robert says I'm being lazy, but it's something else."

"What?"

He shrugged. "Sounds stupid, but I think I'm scared of that point where my neck hits the mat. It might snap or something."

"That doesn't sound stupid, it sounds perfectly reasonable. But you've been scared before, William, and you've always gotten over it."

He smiled. "I remember how terrified I was of doing a round-off. It seems silly." *But now you're going away,* he thought, *and that makes everything different.*

Robert and Mrs. Phillips understood one another. She had attended William's meets ever since he started gymnastics at the age of six. Robert had taught her how to spot William on the more difficult floor exercises, and William knew they both believed in his ability, although they had very different ways of showing it.

When they arrived at the gym, Robert directed Mrs. Phillips to a chair where she had an unobstructed view. The team warmed up and started out with straddle presses on the parallel bars. Then they moved directly to the floor exercises.

"William, we will start with your routine," Robert said. "Don't forget your sense of space. Before you start, you should always know where you are going to land. Are you ready?"

William looked at Mrs. Phillips. She did not smile or nod, but he could feel her concentrating on him. He walked to the corner of the mat, tightened his body, and took a deep breath. The start was slow, with a round-off followed by a whip-back and a layout somersault. By the third pass across the mat, his body and mind were working together, and he knew in that instant, just before the round-off, that he was going to make it. Two flip-flops and both shoulders touched the mat evenly for the dive roll. Up again, tight body, arms outstretched. He was standing just where he wanted to land, two feet from Mrs. Phillips. Her smile was so wide, it seemed to spread from one corner of the gym to the other.

The team burst into applause, but it faded away quickly. Everyone was watching Robert. At last he nodded his approval. "You should come to every practice, Mrs. Phillips," he said, still looking at William. "William only gives us his best when you are here."

* * *

"Robert's right," William said over dinner that night. "I won't be able to do it that well again."

"Why not?" she asked.

"You'll be gone. You won't be there to watch me."

"William, it had nothing to do with me," she said. "It was your mind and your body working together, concentrating on the job you had to do. I'm not your good-luck charm. I don't think you'll believe that until I leave."

They played a game of chess after dinner. He watched her studying the board, lips pursed, chin in her hands.

"Is your head going to fall off?" he asked quietly, and they both smiled at the old joke. When he was younger it had been her way of reminding him to take his elbows off the table.

"Silly bishops," she muttered, glaring at the board. "They just get in the way. I'll give you this one if you like," she offered.

"No way," William replied, grinning. "I know your old tricks. That just clears the way to my queen."

She made a face at him and went back to staring at the board. As he waited for her next move, he turned a pawn over and over in his hand. Its size reminded him of the Silver Knight.

I wish I could hold her in my hand like this, he

thought. *Then she couldn't go away from me.*

He sat up suddenly. He *could* make her small and keep her. Of course, he could. With the token.

All that day and the next, the idea grew inside him until he could think of nothing else. The day before she was supposed to leave, he went up to see the Silver Knight, who was in the stableyard thrusting his dagger into an imaginary enemy.

"You'll be ready for anything when the time comes," William said, settling down next to the castle.

"I do rather hope it comes soon," the knight said, adjusting his belt. "My subjects will have completely forgotten me by the time I return."

"It must be lonely up here all day," William said. "It's too bad I can't visit more often."

"Yes. And a bit of female companionship would not be unwelcome," the knight said. "A lord needs a lady, William."

"Exactly what I've been thinking," William replied gleefully. "And I have just the lady for you."

"Do you, now? And who might that be?"

"Mrs. Phillips. The Lady Elinore. Actually she knows you, although you've never met. She's the one who gave me the castle."

"And is her face fair and are her ways pleasant?"

the knight asked. "I should not like to share my castle with a rough barmaid or a servant girl."

"Very pleasant, my lord. I can't think of anyone better." And what would Mrs. Phillips think of sharing the castle with Sir Simon? William wondered for a moment. He put the thought quickly out of his mind. He would worry about that later.

"All right, then. When will you bring her?"

"Tomorrow night. But I'll need the token. I'll have to do it on the front walk just as she's going to the bus stop. When her back is turned."

"She does not know what you are going to do?"

William hesitated. "No, not exactly. But I'm sure she'll be happy once she's here." The knight was frowning. "Under your protection."

"As Alastor once told me, there is a price to be paid when you meddle with a person's allotted time," the knight said. "She will be leaving your world to come into this one. If she should do that willingly, she may reenter her own world at the exact moment she left. But unwillingly . . ." He shook his head.

"What happens?" William asked.

"She loses time in her own world. Perhaps you could warn her first," the knight suggested hopefully. "Tell her what a strong and honest man I am. I will protect her from any harm."

William's head was whirling. Maybe he should have thought harder about this plan. But there was no time. She was leaving tomorrow. At last, he had what he had wanted all along, the power to keep her with him. He must not let anything change that.

"I'll convince her," William said firmly. "But I want you to come too. I have a special belt pack I use for long bicycle trips. I can carry you downstairs in that. Be ready for me tomorrow afternoon. She's planning to take the four-thirty bus."

That night William sat with Mrs. Phillips while she packed her bag.

"I hate goodbyes," she muttered as she folded layers of tissue paper between her clothes.

"Don't forget this," William said, handing her the photograph from the bureau.

She took it from him with a smile and placed it between the folds of a skirt. "You haven't been fighting to keep me here as hard as I expected," she said. "That's a good sign."

"I haven't given up yet," William said.

"Can you sit on this suitcase for me, William? I can't get it to close. No, don't bounce," she cried. "You might break something."

He slid off the suitcase and opened it. "What's in here?" he asked, lifting off the top layers of clothes.

At the bottom, he found a green wooden box, which he took out and put on the bed.

"I made this for you in woodworking last year. I didn't know you still had it," he said quietly, running his finger along the piano hinge that had been so hard to set in straight.

"I keep my secret things in it," Mrs. Phillips said.

But William wasn't listening. He was thinking, *Wouldn't you like to stay with us forever? Live in a castle with a knight? Never leave?*

"What are you thinking about?" she asked.

"Please don't go," he said one more time.

She put her arms around him and crushed him in one quick hug. "I'm not really leaving, you know. I will always be with you in spirit."

"That's not enough," he cried. He left the room before either of them could say any more.

After breakfast the next morning, William stood awkwardly near the back door while his parents said goodbye to Mrs. Phillips. The grownups were all trying hard not to cry, and it made their voices deep and brusque.

"Please write to us once you get to England," said William's mother. "We want to hear all about your life there."

"You come back and visit us, Mrs. Phillips," said

Mr. Lawrence. He leaned over and gave her a peck on the cheek.

Mrs. Lawrence and Mrs. Phillips hugged each other for a long time. William could see the tears running down his mother's cheeks, and he looked away.

Mrs. Phillips stood at the door and waved them away in the car, as if they were little children leaving for school. When she turned back, she noticed him still standing in the corner.

"You'll be late, William."

He nodded but didn't move.

"Go on, now," she said. "No, I haven't changed my mind and I'm not going to. Don't you see I can't turn back now?" she pleaded.

"Then don't blame me for what happens," he said as he left.

Sir Simon was waiting for William when he climbed up the stairs after school. He could see the small man's body pacing up and down along the wall walk.

"This school of yours takes up entirely too much of your time," the knight exploded as soon as William was in earshot. "When I was a youth, I went to school two mornings a week for some few hours only. There were, after all, more important matters to attend to," he added, glaring at William.

Despite his worries about what was going to happen in the next hour, William had to laugh. "I agree with you completely, Sir Simon, but I don't think my school does. Are you ready to go?"

"Ready? Except for six turns around the courtyard and a quick lunch of mouse legs, I have done nothing but stand here attending upon your lordship. Let us get on with this business. I am eager to see the lady, and I expect she feels the same way."

William let this remark pass.

"I want you to get in here," he explained, unzipping the belt pack he had strapped onto his waist. He helped the knight into it and closed it, leaving a small opening so that Sir Simon could see out.

"Are you comfortable?"

"It will do," came the muffled reply.

Mrs. Phillips's suitcase stood by the back door. William found her in the living room.

"My last tour," she said quickly, her eyes shining. "Quite peculiar, really, to know that I won't see this house again."

"You could come back for a visit," William said.

"It would be too hard. Certain places you must never return to."

She took her dark blue raincoat out of the front hall closet and walked through the kitchen, William trailing along behind. He could hear faint exclamations of surprise from the belt pack, but he ignored them.

"I suppose I'd better get out front, or the bus will leave me," she said.

"I'll take your suitcase," he said, twisting around the kitchen table ahead of her. As he leaned over, he whispered, "Get the token ready, Sir Simon. Do it as she's walking up the path, but make sure you wait until I'm out of the way."

Mrs. Phillips slipped her arm through William's, and they started up the front walk side by side, William slightly bent over with the weight of her suitcase.

"You know how I hate goodbyes," she said, "so I don't want you to wait for the bus. You must write to me. I will be leaving for England in a couple of weeks, after I pack up my apartment. I'll let you know my address when I get there. Remember, you will do well in life because of who you are inside here," she said, giving him a thump on the chest. "A brave, but gentle person. Keep your toes pointed and your body tight for the back handsprings. Believe in yourself, be your own spotter. Now give me a hug and go back into the house."

At the last moment, just as her large arms were encircling him, William remembered Sir Simon and twisted the bottom part of his body to the side. She may have thought he was pulling away from her, because she let him go with a quick kiss. In that awkward moment, he wanted to say, *You're not really leaving, so this hug doesn't matter so much.* But of course, he said nothing, and she took her suitcase and walked stiffly up the path. Forgetting that this wasn't really the end, he stood without moving, imprinting her on his brain. And then she was gone. Completely gone. The token had done its work.

"Sir Simon, where is she?" William cried.

"Down on the ground somewhere, I expect."

"Hold on," William said as he ran forward and dropped to his knees. It didn't take him long to find her, marching stalwartly forward across what was now the great gray expanse of one flagstone, suitcase in hand.

"Mrs. Phillips," he said in a very small voice so as not to startle her. She stopped and turned. "Look up. I'm up here."

"Where am I?" she cried. "Who are you?"

"It's me, it's William." Out of the corner of his eye, William saw a gray flash.

"Sir William, pick her up," cried the voice from his belt pack. "The cat."

William reached down and scooped her up, suitcase and all, just before the neighbor's gray cat pounced on her. Very gently, he lowered her into the belt pack next to Sir Simon. "You explain everything to her," he said to the knight. "I want to get you both back up to the attic before anything else happens."

CHAPTER 8

William walked slowly through the house up to the attic. It would probably take Mrs. Phillips a while to get used to her new arrangement, and he wasn't quite ready to face her. He could barely hear the rise and fall of small voices inside the belt pack. He hoped Sir Simon was doing a good job of explaining the situation to her. He sat down on the top step and waited. The knight was the first to stick his head out.

"Where are we?" he asked.

"Back in the attic," William replied. He put his hand down, palm outstretched, and Sir Simon scrambled on to it. Then the knight turned to help Mrs. Phillips.

"Come, my lady," he called into the darkness of the belt pack. "No need to be afraid. Young William has a remarkably steady hand."

Looking down, William saw her emerge slowly, first the top of her head, the straight white hair rumpled from the trip, then her small arms, still holding her blue raincoat, and finally her small feet in their practical brown walking shoes. Although she'd only known Sir Simon for one short, bumpy ride, she seemed to trust him already. She allowed him to steady her and nodded wearily when he asked her a question in a low voice.

"Hold still," the knight snapped at William. "I understand that you explained nothing at all to her. She is quite shaken. I am going in for her suitcase."

"I'm holding as still as I can," William muttered.

While the small knight fished around for her case, his legs tickling William's palm, she stood without moving or turning around. William looked down at her, but he didn't call out. Small as she now was, she was still Mrs. Phillips, and he could see she was disappointed by the curve of her shoulders.

Sir Simon inched his way back on to the platform of William's hand, pulling the suitcase behind him. "Let's go to the castle, William. I would like to show the Lady Elinore her accommodations."

"She already knows where they are," William said, smiling at the knight, who seemed to have lost ten years in the last hour.

"Ah, but not from the inside," the knight replied.

William lowered the drawbridge and lifted the portcullis for them. Sir Simon helped his companion off William's hand and escorted her across the wooden planks of the bridge, talking and gesturing all the while. When they disappeared around the corner of the outer wall, William lay down on his stomach and waited for them by the entrance. They reappeared from time to time, now at the door of the chapel, now in the front tower. When he saw them head across the courtyard to the kitchen, he lifted the roof off the second floor and watched them come out from the staircase into the master chamber. Mrs. Phillips leaned her head close to the knight's, listening intently to all he had to say. She seemed at home with Sir Simon, which William knew should make him happy, but it didn't. It made him feel oddly lonely.

He sat up so that his face was the right height and distance from theirs. "Do you like it, Mrs. Phillips?" he asked when he saw that the knight had at last come to the end of a sentence.

She stared at him. It was the look of one person trying to recognize another after a long separation. Then she whispered something to Sir Simon and walked off to the other corner of the room.

"William, my lady says she will not speak to you until you restore her to her normal size."

"But Sir Simon, have you told her we can't do that?" William whispered.

The knight put up both his hands as if to warn William off. "There cannot be too many shocks for her at one time," he said quietly. "She thinks this is just temporary and seems resigned to the situation for the moment. Any further revelations would be most unwise right now. I shall make her some dinner and see that she is settled comfortably." He started to move away.

"Wait, Sir Simon," William said. "Tell her—" He stopped. "Tell her I did it because I couldn't stand to have her leave. No, never mind. I'll tell her myself tomorrow. I'm sure she'll speak to me then."

He watched the knight escort Mrs. Phillips toward the tower door, hoping that she'd turn and wave good-bye to him. But of course, she didn't. When Mrs. Phillips made up her mind about something, she rarely changed it. William switched on the small night lamp next to the castle and went downstairs. He wandered through the house, which was darkening quickly with the setting sun.

He stopped at the door of Mrs. Phillips's room. It felt empty, although the smell of her lavender soap lingered in the air. He sat in her chair and looked out her window for a long time, watching the swallows swoop and dip over the lawn in the last, even light of day. "Remember, she isn't gone," he cried out suddenly. "I've still got her with me. Upstairs."

"William? Is that you?" called a voice from the end of the hall.

William jumped up. "Dad?"

His father met him at the door. "It's me. I came home a little early. Has she left?" he asked.

"Yes," William said. He pushed past his father. "Let's go downstairs. It's too dark and creepy up here."

They cooked their favorite meal for dinner that night. William pressed out the waffles with the old black iron, and his father stirred chopped green peppers and Tabasco sauce into an omelet. It was an odd combination of tastes, but over the years they had gotten used to it.

"Was it hard when Mrs. Phillips left?" his father asked as they sat together at the kitchen table.

William nodded. He pretended to concentrate on the maple syrup, filling each separate waffle square before he went on to the next.

"I'm going to try and get home earlier on the nights your mother has evening hours so we can eat dinner together. We'll have to expand our repertoire, though," he said with a smile.

"Well, we still have our pot roast with currant jelly," William reminded him.

"And our chicken soup with bacon bits. But those things take a long time."

"What are you thinking about, Dad?" William asked. "You've got that funny look on your face."

"I thought we'd try Chinese."

"Chinese?"

His father handed William a package from under the table.

"It's an early-birthday–late-goodbye-Mrs.-Phillips present from me. Go ahead, open it."

It was a funny-shaped metal bowl with a Chinese cookbook and two sets of chopsticks inside.

William laughed. "Most fathers give their sons footballs."

His father frowned. "Well, I'm not most fathers and you're not most sons. It's a wok. A special pan for stir-frying Chinese food. We can pick out the recipes the night before, and I'll buy the food on the way home from the office."

"You won't forget?" William asked. The question was a fair one. His father was easily distracted.

"You can call and remind me."

"All right. It's a deal." William started leafing through the book. "For Thursday night, let's do beef and broccoli."

They washed the dishes and put them away. William spread his homework out on the big table in the living room and worked to the blare of Vivaldi's trumpets. His father loved music. Whenever he was in the house, there was music playing in all the rooms on the elaborate speaker system he'd installed himself.

"I've been meaning to get to the attic and measure the castle so I can make the moat," his father said as William headed up the stairs to bed.

"That's all right, Dad," William said nervously. Mrs. Phillips and the Silver Knight would have no warning. "The castle doesn't really need a moat."

"You just think I'm going to give up on this project the way I have on some others."

"I don't mind, Dad. I know how busy you are with everything."

His father smiled and went back to reading the newspaper without another word.

William got into bed without checking on the lord and lady in the attic. He pretended he did not want to wake them, but he knew underneath he could not face her disapproval again. "I'm sure she'll change her mind by tomorrow," he said out loud to nobody. Finally, he fell asleep with the solid lump of his old bear pushed comfortingly against the lump in his stomach.

CHAPTER 9

But she didn't change her mind the next day or the one after that. By Thursday, William had come to dread his afternoon trip to the attic.

"How is she?" he'd ask the Silver Knight, who came up to the upper wall walk at the sound of his footsteps.

"The same," was his inevitable reply. "She is not eating well, and I can hear her pacing long into the night."

William tried everything. In the early morning, he brought her breakfast, small bits of toast sprinkled with butter and Marmite. In the afternoon, when he got home from school, he brought her hot tea. He allowed Sir Simon to light a fire in the fireplace in her bedroom, even though he was worried that the whole castle might go up in flames. He cut curtains for her narrow windows out of some red velvet material from his mother's sewing closet and gave the knight some English postage stamps to paste on her wall. But nothing seemed to work. He had not even seen her since the first day he brought her to the attic.

One afternoon, Sir Simon reported that the giant had been up to visit.

"Which one?" William asked.

"The one you call Dad. He walked all around the castle and then knelt down and spread some ribbon from one corner to the other. Most peculiar behavior. I was watching him through the arrow loop in the wardrobe."

"That was my father. He said he wanted to build a moat for the castle. I wonder if he's really going to do it. Did he see you or Mrs. Phillips?"

"No. He was not here long. I think she considered calling to him for help, but I persuaded her it would be of no use. The only thing that can restore her to her normal size is the other half of the token."

"If only she'd let me explain," William said for the hundredth time.

"She told me last night that she will not come out of her room until you come in and get her," the knight said slowly.

"But she knows I can't do that," William cried. "I'm too big."

There was a brief silence. "I think that's what she means, William," the knight said.

"She wants me to be small too?"

"She wants you to see how it feels."

"But how would I ever get big again? I'd be trapped in there." Even as he said the words, he knew what the knight was thinking. That was exactly what he had done to Mrs. Phillips. "You were part of it too, Sir Simon. It wasn't just my idea."

"We were both too hasty. She was made small against her will, William. There is no changing that now. Every day she spends here, she loses time in her own world. But I have an idea. Meet me by the drawbridge."

William lay down on the floor near the front entranceway to the castle. Slowly, the drawbridge was lowered. Sir Simon walked out to the end of the bridge. Then he turned and pointed up at the riddle written above the castle doors. Once again, William read it.

> When the lady doth ply her needle
> And the lord his sword doth test,
> Then the squire shall cross the drawbridge
> And the time will be right for a quest.

"So what?" he said.

"We have the lord and we have the lady. We are only missing the squire," Sir Simon said. "Think about it, William." Without another word, he went back inside and raised the drawbridge for the night.

The next day, William waited for Jason after school. He needed desperately to talk to somebody. Jason looked surprised to see him.

"Want to bike into town?" William suggested cautiously. "I have to get some food for dinner."

"Sure, I don't have anything better to do." They pulled their bikes out of the rack and headed out to the main road.

"How's the castle?" Jason asked, drawing up alongside.

"Okay. Mrs. Phillips left last week. She said to say goodbye to you."

"I didn't think she was going that quickly."

The traffic was bad, and the two of them had to concentrate on steering for the rest of the ride into town. Jason did seem a bit surprised when William led him through the grocery store to the vegetable section along the rear wall.

"Ginger, broccoli, soy sauce. That's it. We've got the flank steak at home."

"What's the deal?" Jason asked.

"My father and I are cooking Chinese the nights that Mom works late. Want to have dinner with us tonight?"

Jason shook his head. "I'll let you practice for a couple more weeks," he said with a grin.

"Want to come back with me now?"

"Sure."

William was glad he didn't have to talk about his problems right there on the sidewalk. When they got home, he walked through the house turning on the lights.

"I always do that first when I get home," William explained.

Jason nodded. "Must be weird coming home to an empty house after all the years of Mrs. Phillips being here. Kind of neat too. I wish my mother wasn't always hanging around asking about my day at school."

They settled down at the kitchen table with two big bowls of cold cereal.

"Jason, what if you had a friend who really needed your help but you couldn't help him unless you changed yourself," said William.

"What do you mean?"

"Well, pretend somebody was beating me up and your glasses got knocked off and you couldn't find them. Would you try to do something anyway?"

"Sure, but I wouldn't be much help."

"But would you try and fight the guy off anyway?" William asked.

"Well, I wouldn't go away and leave you if you

were in trouble like that."

"That's what I thought you'd say."

"What's this all about?" Jason asked.

William wanted to tell him everything. All about the castle and the Silver Knight and what he'd done to Mrs. Phillips. He knew Jason would not laugh at him, but he also knew that keeping the secret to himself was part of what he had to go through. He'd gotten himself into this mess, and he had to get himself out.

"I'm doing a story for English class and I'm not sure how it's going to end," he said. It was a lame excuse, but Jason didn't question him further.

Maybe when it's all over, I can tell Jason about it, William thought later that night. *When I come back. If I come back.*

He sat up in bed. "If I'm talking about coming back, I must have decided to go," he said to the empty room.

William kept his decision to himself for a couple of days. His visits to the attic were brief and businesslike. He ignored the meaningful looks from the knight and his hints that Mrs. Phillips's health was deteriorating.

On Sunday afternoon when William came in from a special gymnastics practice, his father called him down to his workroom in the cellar. Sitting on the cement floor was a wooden platform, which was surrounded by a separate wooden rectangle.

"Do you like it?" William's father asked.

"What is it?"

"The platform is for the castle. The outer frame is a wall so that when you let down the drawbridge it can rest right here." His father pointed to a notch in the outer wall. "The tunnel in between them is the moat. You take the wall," he said, lifting up the platform.

"Dad, where are you going?" William called.

"Up to the attic." His father's voice floated back to him from the top of the cellar steps.

William picked up the rectangular wall and hurried after him. How was he going to get up there in time to warn Sir Simon?

"Dad, wait, let me go first," he called, but his father was already on the second floor.

"I can't stop now, William. This thing is heavy," he shouted back, and before William could say anything more, he heard the tramp of his father's shoes on the attic steps.

By the time he got upstairs, his father had settled the platform down next to the castle.

"It still smells like smoke up here. I noticed it the other day when I came up to measure the castle," Mr. Lawrence said. "Do you smell it?"

"No," William said quickly. "It's always this way. I'll pick up the castle and you slip the platform under."

"It's too big for you to lift alone," his father said.

"We'll each lift one side and push the platform under with our feet. Ready? Heave-ho."

William lifted his side of the castle very carefully, trying to keep even with his father. Looking down from above, he could see the terrified face of the Silver Knight staring up at him from behind the stable door. Mrs. Phillips was probably in her bedchamber, safely hidden under the roof. They had disturbed Sir Simon's dinner. His plate spilled off the table and rolled across the courtyard while they were pushing the platform into place with their feet.

"All right, let her down, William. There, that's perfect." Mr. Lawrence lowered the outer wall over the castle. "Drop the drawbridge and we'll see how it fits." The drawbridge settled easily into the notch in the wood.

"That's terrific, Dad." William was trying desperately to lure his father back down the steps, but he was pacing around the castle, sniffing the air.

"Odd smell. I don't remember it before. I'd better have a smoke alarm installed up here. Oh, one more part. I have it in my pocket." Mr. Lawrence pulled out a triangular wedge of wood and connected it to the end of the drawbridge. "Now the returning victorious army can get up the ramp."

William stopped worrying about Mrs. Phillips and Sir Simon for a moment. He sat down on the top step and looked up at his father. "Dad, that's the first time you've ever finished a project for me."

"Is it really?" his father said.

"Remember the treehouse that we half built together? And the dog kennel? Well, that wasn't your fault." They both smiled. They'd gotten halfway through the kennel one weekend. When William proudly showed it to Mrs. Phillips on Monday afternoon, she told him she was allergic to dogs.

"And the bookshelves in the cellar," his father added a bit sheepishly. "Never mind. I finished this one."

"That's right. You finished this one and it's great. Just what my castle needed." William stood up.

"Better lift the drawbridge for the night," his father said, leaning over the castle again. "Where is that lever? Oh, here it is."

Please, nobody move, William prayed. The drawbridge seemed to take forever, but at last it was in place.

"It's a very special castle, isn't it?" his father said, looking down on it. "I almost feel as if it's magic in some way."

"It is," William said.

His father didn't ask him to explain. He rested his arm on William's shoulders. "Nice legacy for Mrs. Phillips to leave," he said. "As if her spirit lives on in the attic."

William had a funny feeling in his chest. He knew if he tried to say anything he would start to cry. They stood there a moment longer without speaking.

When William sneaked up later to see if the lord and lady were all right, Sir Simon was pacing back and forth along the wall walk.

"Imagine how you would feel, my boy, if you were sitting down to a nice meal of roasted mouse legs and your entire castle were lifted up and banged about like a mere piece of kindling. I doubt you would take it too kindly. I barely had time to gain the safety of the stable. And Lady Elinore is not herself at all this evening. She has gone to bed early."

"I said I was sorry, Sir Simon. I had no idea my father was coming up here. You have to admit, it's a pretty nice moat and ramp he made."

"A useful contraption, I daresay."

After apologizing a few more times and rearranging the disturbed furniture, William started downstairs. Halfway, he remembered something and came back. The knight was still standing on the wall walk.

"Sir Simon, tell me again about the token. If the person wants to be made small, then time isn't taken away from him, is it?"

"No. The person would return to his world at the same moment he left." The knight looked at William with a strange expression, but he didn't ask any questions.

"Okay, thanks," William said. Their words hung in the air for a moment while neither one moved. William wanted Sir Simon to promise him that if he joined them, he would be sure to come back again. But he knew it was a promise nobody could make to him.

"Good night, William," Sir Simon said at last. "Sleep well."

"Good night."

He had decided he would join them at 4:15 the next afternoon, one week from the moment Mrs. Phillips had been standing on that flagstone looking up at him. He went upstairs right after dinner to pack.

When he'd finally assembled everything on the bed it looked like a very odd assortment. One recorder, one bear, one box of candles, one toothbrush, one jar of Marmite (as a peace offering to Mrs. Phillips), one box of tea bags, four loaves of bread, two bottles of water, one pair of hiking boots, one large box of matches, one pair of binoculars, and a change of clothing. He stuffed everything into a backpack and went to bed.

His mother came up to kiss him good night. She had been on call all weekend, which meant he had barely seen her. She leaned against the headboard with her arm along the back of his pillow. They often took this time to talk at the end of the day.

"Where's Bear? He's usually in on these conversations."

"Down at the bottom of the bed. He's cold." William sighed. Another lie.

"I hear your father gave you the contraption he made for your castle."

"Yes. It's neat."

"How did the practice go this afternoon?"

"All right, I guess. I'm having trouble with the last part of my floor routine. I haven't been able to do it correctly since Mrs. Phillips left."

His mother shifted position to look at him. "I know this week must have been hard for you, adjusting to Mrs. Phillips's being gone."

William looked at his hands. How much easier it would be if that was all he had to adjust to. "I'm tired, Mom. Big day tomorrow."

"All right," she said. "Good night." When she hugged him, he held on to her a moment longer than usual. "You're a great hugger, William," she said as she let him go.

The next day William tried hard to concentrate on his classes so he wouldn't think about what was going to happen to him that afternoon. When he said good-bye to Jason at the end of the day, his friend frowned at him.

"You look kind of funny," Jason said. "You feel all right?"

William nodded. "I guess so. See you."

When he looked back from the corner, Jason was still standing there, his bike leaning against his hip, staring after him.

"Sir Simon," William called softly from the top of the attic steps.

The knight appeared in their customary meeting spot on the wall walk near the south tower. He looked a little weary.

"Good afternoon, William."

"Have you got the token? I'm ready to come."

The knight looked startled. "Ready?"

"Yes. See, I've brought my backpack. I hope I thought of everything."

"But this is wonderful news, William. I must go tell Lady Elinore at once."

"Sir Simon." William put his index finger across the tower door, bringing the small man up short. "Please don't say anything to her. Please just work the magic quickly before I change my mind. I want to do what she asked. I want to go and see her myself."

The small man turned with a new look in his eye. William liked to think it was respect. "Yes, of course. I understand." He reached into his belt pouch. "I'll meet you at the drawbridge."

"Why there?" William asked.

The knight smiled up at him. "At your size, from where you're standing, you can reach the drawbridge with one step. But when you're small, it will take you considerably longer."

The knight disappeared into the south tower to take the stairs. William went and stood at the front entrance of the castle to wait for him. Why couldn't he take back what he'd done to Mrs. Phillips? Then she'd be on her way to England and the Silver Knight could go on his mad quest by himself.

The knight waved up at him from his position by the lever of the drawbridge. When William saw the token held out between the small man's extended hands, he closed his eyes. The hair on his forehead lifted a little in a sudden breeze.

"Do it, Sir Simon. I can't wait forever," he cried.

"It's done," the voice called in reply. William opened his eyes. He was looking up at the gray walls of the castle. He could see the rough lines of mortar between each square stone, the intricate carvings on either side of the doorway, the chiseled letters of the motto above.

Slowly, the drawbridge was lowered, a foot at a

time. William stood watching as the thick planks came down toward him and settled with a thump into the notch of the outer wall. He walked up the ramp his father had made and waited. The bar slid away from its place, and slowly the double doors were opened. Sir Simon appeared at the entrance, his arms outstretched.

"Enter, young William," was all he said.

CHAPTER 10

William hoisted his backpack higher up on his shoulders and walked slowly across the rough wooden planks of the drawbridge. Sir Simon embraced him at the other end as one soldier embraces another.

"No matter what else happens, my boy, nothing shall erase this. You are a courageous person, a squire with the heart and soul of a knight."

William nodded. He didn't dare speak yet, thinking that his voice must have shrunk with his size. Sir Simon lowered the portcullis, and William heard for the first time the squeaky clank of the chains and the deep thud of the pointed wooden spikes as they hit the ground.

"Come. I shall take you to her. We can raise the drawbridge later."

The knight led him across the main courtyard and

into the covered passageway that connected the buttery and the kitchen on one side with the great hall on the other.

"Can we go through this way?" William asked. "I could never see into this room very well from up above." *My voice sounds perfectly all right,* he thought.

Sir Simon nodded and turned left instead of right. The walls of the large banquet hall were hung with intricately woven tapestries. Animal skins of various shapes and colors were spread about on the floors. A long trestle table flanked by two benches took up one whole wall of the large room. William peered into the fireplace, which was as big as his closet at home. Two enormous black pots hung from hooks on one side. Up above, gaily decorated banners were draped over the balcony rail of the minstrels' gallery, but William didn't have time to stop and study them. The knight had already disappeared up the corner staircase. He led William along the wall walk to the curved door in the opposite tower.

"I gave Lady Elinore the master chamber, as I sleep downstairs on the kitchen floor to guard the fire," Sir Simon explained as they stepped on to the landing. "Her room is right through here," he said, indicating the door William was facing. "I shall leave you now."

William stood there for a long moment, listening to Sir Simon's footsteps retreating down the stairs to the kitchen. His heart was thudding in his chest. Mrs. Phillips was humming a tune that sounded vaguely familiar, and he stood for a moment more, listening, hoping it would quiet the pounding in his ears. What if she still refused to speak to him? "Get it over with," he muttered to himself. He knocked.

The humming stopped.

"Sir Simon?" she called.

He didn't answer but turned the hammered metal handle of the door and pushed it open.

She was seated in front of the fire with her back to the door, wearing a long blue robe, covered by some sort of tunic.

"I came," was all he said.

"William," she said. She put down her needlework and stood up.

This time there was no Silver Knight in his belt pack, and he hugged her as hard as he could, his nose buried in the rough linen across her chest.

She pushed him away from her and looked at his face for a long time.

"Do I look different?" he asked.

"No, you look the same." She touched his temple with her forefinger. "It's what's going on here that I wonder about."

"I did warn you. I said I'd make you stay, no matter what."

She went and sat down in front of the fire again. "Then why are you here now?"

"Because I know I made a mistake. I have to go back with Sir Simon and find the other half of the token. The half that sets us free."

He knew she was thinking, *What if you don't find it?* but she didn't say it and neither did he. If he had let himself think what-ifs, he would never have gotten this far.

"Where did you get that dress?" he asked.

"It's actually called a surcoat, and this is a tunic." She fingered the brown cloth on top. "They were hanging in the wardrobe. The castle is very well out-fitted, right down to the pots and pans in the kitchen."

"I brought you some supplies," he said, digging through his backpack. He handed her the jar of Marmite, the bread, and the tea bags. The sight of them made her smile for the first time.

They ate dinner together that night on either side of the table in the courtyard. "Not quite under the stars," Sir Simon said, "but one gets the same feeling." William looked up past the tower walls to where the attic ceiling should have been, but he couldn't quite make it out.

"I'm glad you remembered to leave the lamp on

when you came around to the drawbridge," Sir Simon said.

"The light bulb will burn out eventually," William said, "but I brought candles and matches in my backpack."

"And Marmite," Mrs. Philips said with a smile.

"And good bread," said the knight, tearing off another hunk.

William suddenly felt happy to be there with the two of them, to see them laughing over a joke together at the same table.

"I'm glad I came," he said. They each reached out and took one of his hands.

"It took courage," said Sir Simon. "But you will need more for the days ahead." He stood up. "Tomorrow, my boy, your training begins in earnest."

The next morning the three of them gathered in the courtyard after a hasty breakfast.

First, William was provided with the uniform and weapons of a squire, which the Silver Knight had found in the armory.

"According to the riddle, you must cross the drawbridge as a squire. I will start your training now," Sir Simon explained. He dropped a brown cloth tunic over William's head while murmuring some odd incantation. Then he fastened a belt around his middle, complete with a soft leather bag and a small, sharp dagger in its scabbard.

"What were you whispering?" William asked.

"The words my father said over me when I became a knight: rules of conduct we must respect, be we knight, squire, or page."

"Tell me what they are," William said.

"Be compassionate to the needy. Neither squander wealth nor hoard it. Never lose your sense of shame. If questions are asked of you, answer them frankly but do not ask too many yourself. Be manly and of good cheer. Never kill a foe who is begging for mercy."

"You have forgotten one, Sir Simon," said Mrs. Phillips, who was standing on the side, watching the two of them.

"What is that, my lady?"

"Be ever loyal in love."

He smiled at her. "Oh, yes. But in that one quality, William is not lacking."

"Certain things bear repeating," she replied simply.

"As you wish, my lady."

They divided his training. Sir Simon taught him how to use his dagger, how to improve the speed of his footwork, how to keep his weapons in good order, how to load and fire a crossbow, how to dress and arm his lord, Sir Simon. As it was believed that a knight's strength increases until midday and wanes with the sun, Sir Simon worked with William in the morning and Mrs. Phillips drilled him in the afternoon. They played chess and backgammon. She made him practice his recorder ("Music will calm the beast in man and nature,"), and she put him through his gymnastics exercises.

"Do it again. The round-off wasn't tight enough," she said one afternoon. They had moved the trestle table to the side of the courtyard to make room for his tumbling. Sir Simon sat in one corner, watching while he sharpened the blade of his dagger.

"You're tougher than Robert," William complained as he returned to the starting position.

"Did you go to practice last week?"

"Yes, but Robert said I wasn't paying attention. He wanted you to come back."

She smiled. "You could have brought me in your pocket. Wouldn't Robert have been surprised to see that?"

"There's something else. One day last week, he took me aside at the end of practice. His face was all serious and he said, 'William, when you do gymnastics, you have to be honest about everything you do in the other parts of your life too. Otherwise, your body will deceive you and you won't be able to turn the tricks.'"

"What do you think he meant?" she asked with a smile.

"The thing I had done to you must have been showing through in the floor routine. It's kind of creepy that my own body would give me away like that."

She didn't answer. William did the exercise again. Round-off, two back handsprings, Arabian dive roll.

"Bravo," cried the knight, putting down his dagger to clap.

"Sir Simon," cautioned Mrs. Phillips, "please hold your applause until we are finished. It distracts William, and he needs to concentrate very hard right now."

Sir Simon went back to his work, looking embarrassed. William smiled to himself. He was glad to see somebody else getting in trouble for a change. Mrs. Phillips had been very hard on him all week.

"Now, William, listen to me. I want to alter the routine a bit. The beginning will be the same—round-off, two back handsprings. Then come out of the second back handspring and do an Arabian forward somersault instead of the dive roll."

"You mean a front flip at the end?"

She nodded. He didn't bother to ask why. He knew she would fix him with that steely glare of hers and refuse to answer.

On the first try, he fell in the middle of the front somersault.

"You weren't concentrating," she said. "Your mind was still telling you to do the dive roll. You need to put both mind and body into it. I will spot you for the front somersault this time. Tomorrow you will start doing it yourself."

He was able to execute it perfectly, knowing that her outstretched arm would be there to support his back.

"That's enough for today," she said at last. William glanced over at Sir Simon who raised his fist in a silent cheer behind her back. When she saw the direction of William's eyes, she turned around, but Sir Simon's head was bent close to his work.

"What's all this rehearsing for?" William asked her after the third day.

"You will never be able to defeat the wizard with brute strength," she said. "Let Sir Simon challenge him openly if he wants to. You will have to depend on your brain, your footwork, and the sense of space you have developed as a gymnast. I don't know which of those weapons you will need to use, but all of them must be sharpened just as Sir Simon sharpens his dagger."

"And why the change in the routine to the front flip?" he asked.

"Another weapon. You get back on your feet a little faster that way."

* * *

At the end of a week, Sir Simon declared that they were ready. He and William would leave at dawn.

"I will spend the night alone in the chapel as I did before I became a knight. At daybreak, you must come to me, William, and help me dress."

After the knight left them, William and Mrs. Phillips sat in her room for a long time. In the quiet of the evening, he held himself still, listening for the world outside the castle . . . the world of the attic, of his house, of the traffic going by on the main road. But he couldn't hear anything.

"Do you think it's still there?" he asked her. "Our old world?"

"I'm not sure."

"Will we ever get back?"

"That depends on you."

"Can't you come with me?" he asked, the question that had been at the back of his mind all week. "I still need you to spot me for that final flip."

"Remember what Robert once said to us when he first taught me how to spot you. 'Put your hand out and support him lightly, Mrs. Phillips. Allow William to feel the skill in all parts of his body. You will keep him safe, but he will do the trick.'" She shook her head. "You must find your own way through the forest, William. That's what I've been trying to tell you all along. In this world and our old one. Come stand here by me."

She was seated in front of the fire, doing the same needlework he had seen her with that first afternoon. He had never looked at it closely before.

"What is it?" he asked.

"A firescreen. But that isn't important. Look at the picture."

William leaned closer. "I see a man. There is some-one with him. Someone smaller. And some trees."

Her finger touched the man and then the smaller person. "A man and a boy setting out on an adventure. Into a forest." She glanced up at him. "Remember the motto. When the lady doth ply her needle and the lord doth test his sword. When the squire shall cross the drawbridge . . . Remember?"

He nodded silently. He had forgotten the exact words.

"There are rules in the world of magic just as there are in our world. Everything has its place. Directions must be followed. Each person is given the right weapon. My weapon is the needle and thread."

"Will I be all right?" he asked.

"You are always asking me that question, William. Now I shall ask you. Will you be all right?"

He didn't answer but went over and stood by the

narrow window, looking out into the darkness. To-morrow and the next day and the day after, where would he be? What would he meet?

"I wish you'd never given me the castle. Then you'd be in England and I'd be at home. But now that every-thing is in place, I'm ready to go."

For the first time, the answer came from somewhere deep inside him. And he believed it.

"And whatever happens, you must remember one thing," she said. "That you have within you the weap-ons you need. The heart and soul of a knight in the body of a squire. No other weapon will ever serve you as well as that knowledge."

That night he slept in her room, on a straw pallet in front of the fire.

When he woke up, she was already dressed. She helped him adjust his tunic and slid the soft leather bag along the belt till it hung above his right hip.

"It seems heavier," he said, exploring its lumpy ex-terior with his fingers.

"There's some food in there and your recorder and your binoculars."

"I guess I can't take Bear," he said.

"Your hands must be free, and he's too large to fit into the bag. Anyway, I'll need some company in this drafty old castle. Now go to Sir Simon," she said, crushing him in a quick hug. "I'll meet you in the courtyard."

William slipped both hands through the metal ring of the chapel door and pulled it open. He didn't see Sir Simon at first. He stood at the back, accustoming his eyes to the flickering light from the altar candles and his nose to the sweet smell of incense. An enormous wooden cross filled the dark wall just above the altar. William stared up at it for a long time, held by the sight of the face looking down at him. This dark, holy place with its mysteries and shadows made him feel small and quiet. At last, he saw Sir Simon, lying face down in the main aisle that led to the altar, his arms outstretched. William stayed quiet, waiting. After what seemed like hours, the body moved and Sir Simon clambered slowly to his feet. He passed his squire with a nod, which William took to mean he was to follow in silence.

Sir Simon seemed quieter after his night of fasting and prayer. William remembered his instructions from the week before. First the quilted vest and cap to protect the knight from the hard edges and weight of his own armor. Then the chain-mail shirt with the hood that fastened behind the ears. William had to stand on a stool in order to tie the strings tight enough to suit Sir Simon. Next he strapped on the chest protector and the arm and shoulder guards. On top of the chain-mail leggings, he fastened shin guards to protect the knight's legs from the blow of a misdirected lance. Finally, over the knight's head, he dropped the silver tunic, decorated with Sir Simon's coat of arms; the figure of a lion, flanked by a cross.

"My sword and helmet, William," the knight said at last. "You have done well."

Mrs. Phillips appeared at the side door as Sir Simon was strapping on his scabbard. "I have lowered the drawbridge," she said quietly.

"Thank you, my lady. Since we have no priest, I would ask that you bless my sword."

She stepped forward and touched the carved hilt with her finger. "Remember that you serve both God"—she touched one side of the blade—"and the people"—she touched the other side. "Protect this knight and his squire from any evil that seeks to harm them or keep them from their chosen path."

Sir Simon bowed and slipped the weapon into its sheath. "I would ask of you a keepsake, my lady."

"I am honored, Sir Simon." She took a long silk scarf from her neck and tied it around his forearm.

"And you shall have mine," he murmured as he handed her the token of Janus. "This is for your protection while we are gone. Guard it well," he said as he pressed the leather pouch into her hand. They gazed at one another for a long solemn moment. Then he kissed her hand and turned toward the door.

"Come, William."

William went to her and she kissed him quickly on the forehead. "You will come back," she whispered before she pushed him gently on his way.

As they walked out under the massive stone arch and over the drawbridge, William looked down and saw the muddy waters of a real moat. He reached out to stop Sir Simon and show him, but after a moment's thought he withdrew his hand.

He turned once to wave at Mrs. Phillips, who was still standing under the archway. When he glanced back the second time, the drawbridge had been raised.

CHAPTER 11

The dirt road out of the castle wound around a corner between two rows of stately trees. Summer was in full flower, and the trees seemed weighed down by their heavy green leaves. The dust of the road was damp with the morning dew. Spiders had stretched their webs on the bushes, and drops of water glistened on the strands like tears. Birds chided each other and called out the news of early travelers on the road. Swallows dropped from the trees like stones to snatch a bit of breakfast on the wing.

The day was already warm, and William was grateful for his loose tunic. He and Sir Simon walked in companionable silence for a long time. William wanted to ask where the attic had gone and whether the knight recognized the neighborhood and how he knew which road to take, but he held back his questions. He didn't want to interrupt the knight's meditations.

They stopped for lunch by the side of a wide river, which flowed slowly between high muddy banks.

"The water is low," Sir Simon said. "In the spring, that bridge we just crossed is often washed away by the melting snows."

"You know where we are, then?"

"Oh, yes," Sir Simon said between mouthfuls of bread. "We should reach the edge of my land by noon tomorrow. But we have to go through the forest first. You must stick close by me then."

"Is it dangerous?" William asked.

"It can be," was all the knight replied. He made an effort to get to his feet but was unsuccessful. "Your hand, my squire." William leaped forward and pulled the knight up with both hands, to the clanking of his shin guards. "Oh, I do long for a mount, young William. A true lord does not wish to return to his people walking like a squire."

"Did you have a horse before, Sir Simon?"

"A horse?" the knight thundered. "Our stable was famous for the speed and breeding of our horses, one hundred in all. And I had the best, a silver stallion named Moonlight."

"Is that why you are called the Silver Knight?"

"Yes. When Moonlight and I entered the lists at the

tournaments, the ladies cried with delight. He was the strongest and yet the most graceful of horses. Our bodies moved together as if we were one. Oh, do not remind me of it, William." The knight looked so sad that William changed the subject.

"Let me carry your helmet, Sir Simon. You don't need it yet, do you?"

"No, I expect not. That would lighten my load considerably," he said, handing over the plumed object, which William tucked under his arm.

As they moved away from the river, the land became wilder. The road narrowed with every step. Sir Simon's armor protected him from the thorns of nearby bushes, but William had to stop often to untangle his tunic from their grasp. The song of sparrows had been replaced by the raucous call of the rooks that sat, black and motionless, in the thick trees above them. William had the eerie feeling that the birds were passing word of their progress along to someone ahead.

Sir Simon stopped so suddenly that William bumped into his back. He peeked around the knight to see what lay ahead. The road now looked like a tunnel running into the darkness of the forest.

"My helmet, William. Your hands must be free to reach your dagger. Stay close to me. The forest will be full of the noise of animals. Strange apparitions will tempt you on every side, but no matter what, you must stay on the path. They say that the noise often drives people mad because it is so constant. Talk to yourself if you have to shut it out. Are you ready?"

"Yes," William said. He was pleased that his voice sounded stronger than he felt.

They set off again, more slowly this time. The trees grew close together above their heads. Even though the sun was still high in the western half of the sky, it seemed as if night had already fallen. Once William looked behind him, but the road had turned a corner and he couldn't see where they'd entered the forest. Small animals rustled and stirred in the undergrowth, and more than once, William felt a warm, furry body rush by his legs. The view ahead was blocked by the clanking silver form of his companion. William wondered how Sir Simon could possibly see which way the path went in the darkness. It seemed to twist and turn about until William had lost all sense of direction.

He tried to duck away from the branches that slapped back in Sir Simon's wake, but often they caught him full in the face, raking his cheeks with their claws and poking him in the eyes. The cry of the rooks mingled with strange growls and snarls on all sides, so that the noises around them became as thick as the forest itself. Just when William thought he couldn't stand it any longer, he saw a spot of light.

"Sir Simon," he cried. "Look. It must be the way out."

The knight stopped. "Close your eyes, William," he said, his voice echoing from inside the helmet. "It is only a trick to tempt you off the path."

William obeyed, and when he looked the next time, the spot was gone and darkness had closed down around them again.

They stumbled on for what seemed like hours. William's feet hurt, and the scratches on his face and his arms had begun to sting. Meanwhile, the noises grew more intense with every step. William kept his hands over his ears whenever he could.

Neither of them had eaten or drunk anything since their stop by the river, and he longed for a drink of water. The more he tried to forget about his thirst, the more desperate he became. Suddenly, above the animal noises, he could distinguish the gurgling of a stream off to his left. He peered in the direction of the noise, and in the murky darkness he saw the glint of silver water as it fell over stones. *Surely, this isn't an apparition*, he thought. The stream turned and ran close by their feet. *I'll stop to take a drink*, he said to himself. *I need the feel of water on my tongue for a moment*. He stooped down, and in an instant he felt Sir Simon's hands roughly pulling him back.

"I just wanted a little drink," he cried.

"Shut your eyes, William," the knight whispered. William could feel the cold steel of Sir Simon's helmet next to his cheek. "Do as I say," he ordered again. William obeyed. They stayed that way until William had gathered enough strength to resist the gurgling stream. When he struggled to his feet, it was gone.

"I'm sorry, Sir Simon," he said.

The knight patted him clumsily on the shoulder, and they started down the path once more. William had to concentrate very hard on lifting one foot, putting it down again, lifting the other. Every now and then, he reached up and touched the knight's back for reassurance.

He was shaken out of his dreamlike walk by a joyful cry from inside the knight's helmet. Only one word. "Moonlight." Before William could stop him, the knight had plunged into the forest after a silver horse that William couldn't see. It was only the knight's warning about the path that kept William from rushing after him.

"Sir Simon," William cried. "Don't leave me." He called over and over again into the darkness in case his voice might lead the knight back to the path. At last, when his voice grew hoarse and he was too tired to stand, he sank to the ground and cried until he fell asleep.

* * *

When William woke, he sat up slowly, stiff from his cramped position between the two thick roots of a tree. It was impossible to tell the time of day because of the darkness in the forest. The noises, which seemed quieter at first, began to grow in intensity again, as if the animals had been gathering strength while he slept.

He slid open the strings of his leather pouch and pulled out an apple and another hunk of bread. As he sat there, biting into the sweet, crisp fruit, he thought about Sir Simon. Maybe the knight had stumbled back to the path a little farther on and they'd meet when William found his way out of the forest. The thought cheered him, and he pulled himself to his feet. After hopping up and down a bit to get the blood moving through his legs, he set off, watching carefully for the dim outlines of the path.

The juice of the apple had helped quench his thirst, but it was hard going without Sir Simon's silver shape to guide him. He stopped once or twice to make sure he was still on the path. What if he stumbled off? There would be nobody to pull him back, nobody to come looking for him. He would wander around in this forest forever, until he died of starvation or went completely crazy from the noise. The noise. The cacklings mingled with roars, grunts, groans, moans, the scream of a hyena, the far-off whistle of a bird.

All around him, he heard the beating of animals in the underbrush, and he imagined their claws reaching out to scrape his unprotected legs, their sharp fangs. . . . "Be quiet," he screamed, but there was no relief. He sat down again to rest.

He wanted to give up, to stay there forever with his hands pressed over his ears. Anything to lessen the noise. Suddenly he remembered the recorder. He knew the thin, reedy notes were not loud enough to drown out the animals, but if he could just listen to something else for a while, he might be able to go on.

He pulled the recorder out, ran his tongue over his lips, and blew a couple of notes. The silence was instantaneous, but as soon as he stopped playing, the noises began again, slowly at first and then building up. He played five more notes. Silence.

"Well, now," he said, feeling much happier. "I've never had such a good audience. Any requests?" His voice was drowned by the growing roars and growls. But when the animals heard the notes of his recorder, they kept still.

William walked along, his eyes on the path, playing every song he had ever learned. "Hot Cross Buns." "Scarborough Fair." "Michael Rowed the Boat Ashore." After a while, he started on Christmas carols. "Away in a Manger." "Silent Night." The familiar tunes made him think of home, of the tinsel-covered tree they always set up in the corner by the bookshelf, of the first snowfall, when he and Mrs. Phillips always made a snowman with a carrot nose and two pine cones for ears.

Slowly he became aware of the gloom lifting ahead of him, but he didn't dare look too closely in case he was being tempted again. When he did at last glance up, he could see blue sky through the twisted branches of the trees. After a few more songs, the road led him out into the middle of a large field.

William slipped his recorder into his pouch and turned a cartwheel right there in the middle of the road. "I did it," he cried. "I made it through the forest all by myself." Then he turned two more cartwheels and a front handspring to congratulate himself once more.

"Not bad," said a voice from the side of the road.

William pulled his tunic down and straightened his dagger while he looked for the speaker. At last, he saw a small boy sitting on a stone wall. His head was topped with a circle of blond hair, and he was whittling a stick with lazy strokes.

"Good morning. I didn't know anybody was watching me," said William.

"Not many travelers make it through the forest alone," the boy said.

"Actually, I was with someone, but he . . . he took a different path," William said. "Have you seen him?"

"No," said the boy. "And I expect I never will. There's only one path through the forest, and you were on it."

William decided to say no more about Sir Simon. "I'm looking for the castle of the wizard Alastor. Can you tell me how to get there?"

"You'd do better to go back into the dark forest," the boy said casually. "Everybody else I've seen is trying to get away from Alastor."

"I have important business with him," William said, standing as straight as he could.

The boy looked him up and down and shrugged. "From what I hear, Alastor only does business with the devil, but suit yourself." He cocked his head to the right. "Follow this road and you'll find your way soon enough. The wizard has left his mark on the land."

"Thank you," William said, starting off in the direction the boy had indicated. "If you see my friend, will you tell him which way I've gone?"

"What's he look like?" the boy asked.

"He's a knight with a silver helmet."

At that, the boy scrambled off the fence. He ran up to William and looked around him quickly before speaking again. "You mean the Silver Knight has come back?" he whispered, holding on to William with both hands.

William didn't answer right away. "What's it to you?"

"My grandmother was the Silver Knight's nurse when he was a baby. We know that Alastor defeated him with magic, but my mother says he will return and take back his kingdom. Then our troubles will be over."

"What troubles?" William asked.

"Ever since Alastor made himself lord, the crops have not grown well. The animals have gotten sick and died. The cows haven't given milk. Even the wells have gone dry. They say that Alastor has a storeroom of gold in the castle, but each year he demands higher and higher rents from us. People disappear in the middle of the night, and we never see them again." The boy stopped his frenzied whispering and glanced about him. "They say everybody is Alastor's spy."

William could see the fear dancing in the little boy's eyes, and a shiver ran down his back.

"Can I trust you?"

"I told you the story of Alastor, didn't I?" the boy said.

"All right, then. You must stay here and wait for the Silver Knight. Tell him I have gone ahead and shall meet him at the castle. Tell him he must disguise himself so that Alastor doesn't know he's coming."

William pulled the boy's hands. "You mustn't tell anyone that he's near. Do you hear me? No one. If Alastor is warned . . ."

But William didn't need to say more. The boy's expression had changed again.

"It's no use," he said. "If he went off the path, he'll never find his way through the forest. Nobody ever has before. And you won't be able to defeat Alastor on your own."

"I came through the forest on my own," William said. The boy didn't seem to be listening. "I have to get on my way. Remember what I told you," he called from the top of the next rise, but the boy had already climbed back to his post on the stone wall. He didn't even raise his hand to wave goodbye.

CHAPTER 12

William stomped rapidly over the next two hills, eager to put as much distance as possible between himself and the forest. The dust rose with each footstep, and he looked around for some sign of water. Although it was full summer, only a few ears of corn and some stunted grain grew in the dry brown fields. He saw people in the distance standing idly about, watching him. Someone moving briskly across the landscape at any hour was obviously an object of interest.

"Hey, there," he called to one young man. "Where can I find some water?"

The man pointed further down the road and turned away quickly. When William glanced back over his shoulder, the man was watching him. Around the next corner, he came to a bridge that crossed what must once have been a pleasant stream. The water had dried up in all but the deepest pools, but William was so thirsty, he lay down in the dry streambed and put his face in a puddle. The water tasted brackish, and he took only enough to wet his mouth.

He knew by the position of the sun that it was early afternoon, and he pressed on even though his legs had begun to tire. He longed to lie in the cool shade of a tree for an hour or so. He didn't know why he was in such a terrible hurry because, with the Silver Knight gone, he had no plan to defeat the wizard. In fact, when he thought about it, he wondered whether Sir Simon had ever had a plan himself. The knight acted as if he could march right up to the castle door in a full suit of armor and run the wizard through with his sword. But all Sir Simon's sharp weapons and long hours of training had done him no good the first time, so why would they work now? And if a well-trained knight with a sword and a helmet could be turned to lead, what would happen to a mere squire with a puny dagger and a quaking heart?

William was striding along, thinking all these things over, when someone called to him. He looked up to see an old man sitting on a rock under a tree.

"Young fellow, come over here, will you?"

William hesitated. He wanted to reach the castle that day if possible, and he didn't want to hear any more terrible stories about the power of the wizard.

"I'm awfully sorry, but I'm in a hurry," he called, taking a few more steps. The man looked sad at the sight of William moving away so quickly.

"I need your help," he said.

William turned back and looked more closely at the man. He was dressed in the shreds of a long tunic, and the surface of his face was as wrinkled as the skin of an old apple.

Be compassionate to the needy, said Sir Simon's code. William supposed his quest could wait a few minutes.

"How can I help you, sir?"

The man leaned backward and looked up the tree, which was quite difficult for him, as the upper part of his body was curved over his lap so that his nose almost touched his knees. William had the feeling he might tip off his perch and roll way. "Do you see that apple way at the very top?" he asked.

William looked up. This apple tree seemed taller than most. Its leaves hung down, limp and dusty, as if exhausted by the length and heat of the summer. From the highest branch hung one dark apple.

"Yes, I see it," William said.

"Could you climb up there and pick it for me, young fellow? I have not eaten since yesterday, and the emptiness in my stomach has begun to pain me terribly."

"I have a little bit of bread I could give you."

"No, my boy, I'm afraid only the apple will do." He sounded so sad when he said this that William had the feeling he had said it before. William grasped the lowest branch and hoisted himself up.

The old man spoke again. "Remember, boy, while you are climbing you must not look down or you will never reach the top. And when you get the apple, do not take a bite of it or both of us will always go hungry."

William did not reply. Everybody in this country seemed eager to tell him not only what to do but how to do it.

At first, he rather enjoyed the climb. It was breezy this high off the ground, and William stopped once or twice to look at the countryside. He could see his road curving off across a series of pastures. In the distance, he thought he saw the towers of a castle, but it was hard to make them out because much of the horizon was covered by a long black cloud of smoke. He glanced up every now and then, but the apple didn't seem to be getting any closer.

"This is the tallest tree I've ever climbed in my life," he said out loud just to keep himself company. His voice startled two birds, who flew away in a rush. "If I could fell this tree and lay it on its side, I'd be halfway to the castle by now."

He stopped again to catch his breath. He was about

to look down when he remembered what the old man had said. "Sir Simon," he cried. "Where are you now that I really need you?" The thought of his friend plunging endlessly through the dark forest kept him staring at the sky. *Follow the rules. Don't look down. Don't stray off the path.*

The upper branches of the tree were thin and delicate. They swayed in the lightest breeze. William had to concentrate very hard on the dark red circle at the top to force himself up the rest of the way. The apple came off easily in his hand, and when he had maneuvered down to the sturdier branches, he stopped to study it.

Never had he seen an apple with such a smooth, dark skin or felt such firm flesh. He longed for a bite. His last drink had been the stagnant water in the streambed, and this endless climb in the sun had made the sweat stand out on his face and neck. Surely one little bite wouldn't hurt. He had just opened his mouth and put the dark, firm skin against his teeth when he saw two birds flying toward the tree. They were coming right for him, and he had to scamper down to the next branch to get out of their way. He put the apple back to his mouth when, with a babble of chirps, they came for him again.

He ducked. "All right, all right," he shouted. "I

know I'm not supposed to eat it."

To distract himself from the apple, he half climbed, half slid down the tree at a terrific rate. He reached the bottom in much less time than it had taken him to climb to the top.

The old man snatched the apple from him with a cry of joy and took an enormous bite. Before William's eyes, his twisted old shape was transformed into the tall, straight body of a young man, who threw his arms around William and gave him a bone-crushing hug. Then the two strong arms pushed the boy away and shook him a bit. William felt like an old sack.

"You have broken the wizard's spell for me," cried this new person who could not stop clapping William on the back.

"All I did was bring you the apple," William said. "Please, sir, could I have a bite of it? I haven't drunk anything since early this morning, and the hot climb made me thirsty."

But to William's horror, the young man threw the apple as far into the field as he could. "You must not bite that apple, for it has a spell on it. But do not worry. I have something else for you to eat, and anything that is mine, you are welcome to."

With that, he reached into a sack under the bench and produced a series of small bundles wrapped in rags.

In just a few minutes, he had spread a picnic of bread and cheese and dark cider beneath the tree. "Set to, my boy."

The young man stared intently at William while he ate. William began to squirm under his gaze.

"Please, don't look at me that way, sir. I didn't do anything special. I would have bitten into the apple if the birds had not warned me away from it."

"Not many people have bothered to stop and listen to my request, and only one went up the tree. He looked down and was never seen again." The young man stood up and stretched. "It feels good to have my own body back. I have been imprisoned inside that old man's shape for years."

"Why did the wizard put the spell on you?"

"I was caught stealing apples. My baby boy was very sick, and the doctor said he must eat apples every day to cure his disease. The orchards were already wasting away. The wizard's servant caught me stealing a bag of apples from his storeroom, and Alastor put this spell on me. That was in the old days when he amused himself by making up new and interesting spells. I understand that now he is bored and grumpy with his life, and he just uses the old spell that always worked best."

"And what's that?" William asked.

"He turns everybody to lead. He keeps the important people or the beautiful maidens or the particularly bad villains in a special gallery so that he can admire them whenever he wishes." The man shrugged. "But they say even that does not keep him amused anymore, so he is searching for a fool to entertain him. Of course, nobody has applied for the job, but if one doesn't come forward soon, Alastor will send his men out into the countryside to find one. Woe to that poor fellow, whoever he is."

By this time, William had finished most of the food that had been set before him. "I don't seem to have left you much," he said. "I didn't realize how hungry I was."

The man laughed. "That one bite of the apple will suffice me for a long time. Pack up the rest and take it with you. Where are you headed?"

"The wizard's castle," William said quietly.

"Oh, no, my boy, you cannot go there. Come along with me. I am going back to search for my wife and child to take them out of this accursed land. Join us."

"I'd like to, but I can't. I must go my own way."

"You know, of course, that a dragon guards the gate to the castle," said the young man.

"No, but I did see a cloud of black smoke on the horizon when I went up the tree."

"The land around the castle is parched from his fiery breath. You must give up your foolish plan. Nobody can pass into the castle without Alastor's permission."

"Thanks to you, I have an idea. Alastor is looking for a fool, and I'm an acrobat. I can play my recorder and turn some cartwheels. Perhaps that will help get me into the castle."

"In some ways, you *are* quite the fool, my boy. But if you are so determined to go, let me tell you a little secret I learned when I was younger. My wife's mother was Calendar, the nurse to Simon, the king's son. When Alastor first came to the kingdom, she used to spy on him to learn his secrets. He paid her no notice, thinking her a foolish old woman. She came out of the castle only once after Sir Simon was defeated and sent away. Alastor had begun his 'reforms,' and the people were already beginning to suffer under his rule. Soon after Sir Simon left, the wizard set a dragon at the gates of the castle to guard him against attack. That dragon was Calendar's cat, transformed. On that last trip out of the castle, Calendar looked haggard and worn. Her body was bent over, much like mine was just an hour ago, and in her eyes there was a haunted look, as if she had seen miseries beyond telling. 'Alastor will not let me come again, Dick,' she said. 'But I will tell you what I know now.'

"Then she told me how to defeat the dragon. As long as you look directly into his eyes, the dragon's fire cannot harm you. The most horrible scenes will be reflected in his eyes, and you will want to look away. But you must resist, because if you avoid looking at him, you are finished. Keep telling yourself they are only illusions. When you get close enough, plunge your dagger into his right thigh. That is the only place where the blade will sink in. Then he will be under your control. Do you understand?"

William nodded wearily. There seemed to be so many things to remember, so much to overcome, and he hadn't even reached the castle yet. He got to his feet and packed away the food in his leather pouch.

"I must be off," he said. "Thank you for your help. I have good news for you too. I have met your son. He greeted me when I came out of the forest. He is alive and well."

"How do you know he is my son?" Dick asked, grasping William by the arm.

"He told me that his grandmother was the Silver Knight's nurse."

"So you know Sir Simon was called the Silver Knight? This is too much." The young man stepped back and eyed William once more. "There is a legend . . . ," he muttered to himself. "About a boy."

Then he shook his head. "It cannot be." He walked with William up the road a bit. "Good fortune to you," he said. And he stood there waving until William turned the corner.

CHAPTER 13

For the rest of the afternoon, William plodded steadily up the road against a constant stream of people going the other way. He kept his head down to avoid the curious stares and the warnings to turn around. He couldn't help overhearing other snatches of conversations that disturbed him.

"What did he do to the man?"

"Turned him to lead. I saw it with my very eyes. Same as he does to everyone."

"And the boy too?"

"The boy too. The soldiers picked them both up and carried them away."

"There's no use staying here anymore. He was the one we were waiting for, and he's been destroyed just like all the others."

"It's a terrible thing." This last remark was greeted with low murmurs of assent.

William put his hands over his ears. They couldn't mean the Silver Knight. If he let himself believe that, he would lie down in the middle of the road and give up. So he took the thought right out of his mind and left it sitting there on the side of the road.

William arrived in the vicinity of the castle just as the sun was setting. Even before he reached the castle itself, he knew he was getting close because the land was becoming more and more parched. The houses looked abandoned, and the last people he passed were driving their small herds of scrawny goats and pigs along ahead of them. William could practically count the animals' ribs.

"You don't want to go that way," an old woman called out to him. "You'd do best to turn around and come with us. We're all leaving."

William begged for a little water and continued on his way despite their urgings.

In the distance, the sky was a dull gray color, and large pieces of ash floated past him on the hot breezes. William came around the last corner, and there stood the castle, towering above him at the top of a rise. He could see the soldiers patrolling the upper battlements, so he ducked behind a tree. The site had been well chosen, a rocky hill with a path that curled back and forth until it reached the top. A tower stood at each corner, and arrow windows dotted the exterior walls in a random pattern. A single black pennant flew from the corner of one tower. William pulled out his binoculars and focused in on the main gate.

The dragon, a brownish-green, scaly creature, prowled in front of the double wooden doors, endlessly turning on himself so that the occasional bursts of flame from his mouth barely missed his tail. As William watched, the dragon spied a bird that had flown too close, and he shot his tongue of flame high into the sky. The bird dropped like a stone.

William shuddered. He stood without moving, remembering the time he had picked up the waffle iron without a potholder. The pain of the burn was with him for days afterward. But he could put down the waffle iron. Once he started walking toward the dragon, there would be no turning back.

William put away the binoculars and began to look around quickly for a place to spend the night. The heat that the dragon discharged into the air had withered away much of the undergrowth. Finally, he found shelter under some lower bushes a short distance from the road.

He couldn't eat. The sight of the dragon had taken away his appetite. He lay curled under the bushes, listening to the occasional crackling of the dry under-growth. No bird sang, no night-prowling animal called out. He felt very small and very much alone.

"The noises of the dark forest were better than this," he said out loud. The sound of his own voice reminded him that he had himself, after all.

He talked to Mrs. Phillips even though she wasn't there. "Are you weaving the story? Have you seen the forest and the apple-tree man? I guess the dragon is just beginning to appear on the tapestry. If I don't succeed, does it mean you won't know where to put the needle next?" The thought silenced him for a moment. "Oh, please, help me," he whispered to the night. There was no answer.

The heat woke William before daybreak. He took a couple of bites of bread and set off for the castle. When he stopped to look through the binoculars, he could see the soldiers jabbering to one another and pointing down at him, but no arrows were sent his way, no jars of boiling oil were tipped over the walls. He had to laugh at his own foolishness. When you had a dragon guarding the gates, what need was there for crossbows and oil?

The heat become gradually more intense. He longed to strip off his tunic, but it didn't seem wise to approach a dragon in a shirt and leggings. He stopped and leaned on the last tree to pull himself together.

He was terrified. The palms of his hands were wet and clammy from nerves, not the dragon's heat. The dragon had stopped his pacing. He lifted his green head and sniffed the air. Out rolled his tongue, an immense carpet of red that furled into the sky and back into the black hole of his mouth.

William stood, staring. He turned his back on the dreadful scene and began to walk away down the road. "I'm sorry," he said to nobody. "I can't do it. I'm too small and afraid." But he had not gone far before his steps slowed and stopped. He turned and looked again at the dragon. "Mrs. Phillips," he whispered, "are you listening? What weapon do I use for this?" He held himself as still as possible, half hoping to hear her soft voice in his ear, but nothing came to him.

He put his hand into his pouch and ran his fingers over the binoculars, a last bit of bread, the recorder. Pulling out the wooden instrument, he put it up to his lips and blew a single clear note. The music had soothed the wild pounding of his heart before. Maybe it would work again.

He actually felt relieved when he stepped away from the tree and faced the beast head on. The dragon looked stunned by the arrival of this rather small, not very well armed opponent, and he held his fire while sizing him up. William drew out his dagger with one hand and put the recorder back to his lips.

He began to play "The Battle Hymn of the Republic" and started forward, one foot after the other, his eyes at last locked with the dragon's. When the first blast of fire hit him, the flames seemed to separate and coil around him. Four more steps and his wooden recorder grew hot to the touch. *Mine eyes have seen the glory of the coming of the Lord.* The eyes of the dragon grew larger like enormous mirrors. In their reflection, William could see his image replaced by the crater of an erupting volcano. Just when the circle of fire was large enough to swallow him up, the picture in the dragon's eyes changed again. Now William was forced to watch a house burning. People were leaning out of the top windows, screaming for help. He was desperate to shield his eyes from the look of misery and terror on their faces, but in the midst of the tumult he heard the music, still winding its way out of his recorder. *His truth is marching on.*

Another curling blast of fire combined with a roar of anguished fury filled the air. William began to falter. He longed to look away, to lose himself in the great immensity of an ocean or the cool sweep of the sky above them, but the words of the apple-tree man rang in his ears: "Keep telling yourself they are only illusions."

The scene in the dragon's eyes changed again, and

this one was the worst. It showed Mrs. Phillips sitting in her bedroom by the fire working on her needlepoint. She didn't see the spark that landed on her robe, but William did. "Watch out," he screamed, pulling the recorder from his mouth, but she couldn't hear him. By the time she saw the small flames, it was too late, and he had to watch her beating at them with her hands, trying to shield her face as they climbed like living snakes up her tunic. *The music, William,* a voice said inside his head. He put the recorder back to his lips and played again. *We have seen Him in the watchfires of a hundred circling camps.*

He took three more faltering steps into the center of hell. The dragon's eyes went black, and William felt his hand brush against the rough scales of the beast's hide. He reached up with his dagger and plunged it in the direction of the right thigh. Nothing. Air. The noise of the dragon's roar was deafening, and William staggered back. He flung out his arm and struck one more time. At last, the dagger found flesh and was slowly pulled from his hand as the beast fell over on to his side in a heap of green scales. William sank to his knees in the dirt and let the recorder drop from his mouth.

Neither of them moved for a moment. In the silence and the settling dust, William could hear the high clear note of a bird's song. He closed his eyes and waited for the pounding in his chest to subside. Then he forced himself to look once more into the dragon's eyes.

This time there were no scenes of fiery horror but only the terrified and lonely eyes of the cat imprisoned inside this grotesque green body. There was no blood. There was not even a wound. The dragon was not lying there in pain.

"Come on, now, you must get up," William said. "I'm not going to hurt you."

The dragon began to struggle, moving his legs about under him in useless, scrabbling circles. His forelegs were much shorter than his back ones, so it was hard for him to get them all organized underneath him. William went around on the other side and pushed hard, which got the dragon balanced again. Slowly he righted himself and stood up. He hung his head down with a sniff and pretended to be inspecting the dusty road.

"Don't be like that," William said. "You put up a good fight. Now I need your help. We don't want the wizard to know that you're in my power. You've got to keep standing here and guarding the gates as if nothing has happened."

The dragon looked up hopefully. He opened his mouth and spat a bit of flame to the side.

"That's right," William said with a smile. "A puff here or there, but you're not to hurt anybody who approaches the castle gates. Do you understand?"

The dragon nodded and took up his old position.
William glanced at the ramparts. The soldiers were
clustered together, whispering and pointing at him fear-
fully. When they saw him looking up, they fell silent.
William waved and then, with an exaggerated gesture,
put his finger to his lips. He knew he was taking a
chance, but if the wizard's soldiers had been pressed
unfairly into his service, they might keep the secret of
the dragon.

He retrieved his dagger from where it lay in the dust
and hid it under his tunic. Then he marched across
the drawbridge right up to the door and knocked loudly
three times.

CHAPTER 14

William heard the crank of the windlass as the portcullis was raised. The heavy wooden doors were pushed slowly open by two soldiers, who marched across in front of him without raising their eyes to meet his. A third soldier stood waiting for him, lance at the ready.

"Your business, sir?" he said.

"I've heard the wizard is seeking a fool for his amusement. I've come to apply for the position," William said loudly, his voice echoing throughout the empty courtyard. Here and there he spied faces peeking out at him from behind the great stone columns, but when they caught him looking at them, they withdrew.

The guard signaled that William was to follow him. They took the first door that led off the courtyard and turned their way down an endless spiral of stairs that seemed to lead into the center of the earth. The stairs were lit by smoking torches that left long black marks on the stone walls above them. For the first time since he'd come through the forest, William felt cold. He was glad he had not shed his tunic in the heat. The guard did not look back to see if he was still following but kept up a steady pace down the curling stone steps. At last, when William began to grow dizzy from the downward twisting and the acrid smell of the torches, they came out into a small room.

"Wait here," the guard said. He knocked once and then twice more at a wooden door, which was opened almost immediately and then slammed shut behind him. William was left standing by himself, but in less than a minute the door opened a crack. A bony hand reached out and beckoned him inside. He entered a large hallway dimly lit by two torches on either side of a high-backed carved chair.

"Step forward, fool," thundered the figure seated on the chair.

William did as he was told. He found himself face to face with an old man, dressed in a silver robe with a hood. They studied each other in silence. Lines creased the man's forehead, and his gray hair lay across the shiny skin of his head in thin, matted strands. His right shoulder twitched constantly as if it were jerking up to swat a fly off his ear. His eyes made William shiver. They darted about, never resting for too long on any one object. They were the eyes of a hunted man who understood that danger could come from any quarter. They missed nothing.

"I am Alastor," the man announced. "Your name, fool?"

"Muggins," William replied. It was the first word that came into his head, the name of a clown he'd once seen in the circus.

"What can you do?" the wizard asked, leaning forward to look more closely at his face.

"I am an acrobat, sir. I can play the recorder. I can tell riddles." William stopped as the wizard made an impatient gesture at him.

"Enough," he growled. "That will do, won't it, Calendar?"

"Aye, my lord," croaked a voice from the corner, and William looked over to see the bent shape of an old woman. "Order him to perform," she said.

The wizard nodded at him. William stepped back to the entrance of the room. He would use the beginning of his routine for the meet. But no Arabians. He wasn't ready for that. For a moment, he stood with his eyes closed, centering his body. He thought of Robert's voice. To succeed, William knew that everything else—the smoky room, the wizard's angry eyes, the guards' curious stares—had to drop away.

"Perform, fool," the wizard ordered, his deep voice bouncing off the walls of the room.

Ready, go . . . round off, whip back, reach for the back handspring, he had the rhythm and the speed for the second pass. Another round-off, then a perfect layout somersault with a full twist, which was ruined only by the clatter of his falling dagger. The guard leaped forward and snatched it from the floor before William could retrieve it himself.

"Most interesting," the wizard said. "A fool who travels with a dagger." William said nothing. He was sure the wizard could hear the pounding of his heart, but he did not let the fear show in his face. "What do you think, Calendar?" asked the wizard.

The old woman shuffled forward and inspected the weapon, putting it up to her nose and sniffing it. "No blood," she muttered, handing it back to her master. "But how did he get past the dragon?"

"Well, fool, you heard the question," the wizard muttered.

William opened his mouth and shut it again. He had no idea what to answer. He stared at his feet, hoping they would help him decide which answer was the safest one.

Before he spoke, he heard the soldier's voice behind him.

"When he stated his business, we directed him to

the side entrance, my lord. We knew you were looking for a fool."

The wizard's eyes came to rest for a moment on the soldier. Nobody in the room moved.

"Very well, then. We shall keep the dagger for you, young Muggins," the wizard said. "That way you won't be tempted to use it, will you?"

"No, sir," William ventured warily.

"Come with me, fool. I have something to show you."

William picked up his belt and followed the silver robes. They reminded him for a moment of Sir Simon, but again he shook the thought away. Calendar scuttled along behind them, sniffing at him occasionally like a curious dog. They went out a back door behind the wizard's chair, down a sloping, narrow corridor, and through a series of stoutly fastened doors, each opened by a guard and closed again behind them. At last, they arrived in a large gallery hall whose walls were lined with statues.

"These are my pets," the wizard said with an eerie smile. "Take a closer look at them, fool."

This was the room that William had heard about, the place where the wizard displayed his lead people. William walked slowly around the edges of the room, forcing himself to look into each face. He saw old men and children, fearful faces and kind ones, wide, staring eyes, arrested in the middle of a plea or a protest or a prayer. The wizard was talking to him, boasting about some of his best prizes, a visiting prince and a wily priest. When William came to the last two figures, he put his hand over his mouth to stifle his scream of horror. It was the Silver Knight and the son of the apple-tree man. So the whispers he had heard on the road were true. His beloved Sir Simon had been defeated again. When the wizard came and stood beside him, William held himself very still. Even in the midst of his despair, he knew he must mask the fear and fury that raged within him.

"This is my most recent prize, an old enemy who has tried to take my kingdom before. It was rumored that he would return one day with a boy, and so he has. But neither one of them shall bother me again," Alastor crowed. "The Silver Knight has been defeated, and in honor of his destruction, I have chosen to wear silver myself."

At that moment he put his hand up to his neck, and William caught a glimpse of the two medals hanging from the necklace. There at last was the token, the prize he had come all this way to get. It was so close now that he toyed with the idea of reaching up and snatching the medal from around the wizard's neck before anybody could stop him. Could he do it? He glanced about the room. The two guards standing at the door saw his look and took a step forward with their lances ready. He would have to bide his time.

The old wizard fingered the woven ribbon nervously for a moment and then tucked it out of sight again as if he could read William's mind. "You stole one of my precious little treasures from me, but I shall have it back someday," Alastor said, speaking now to Sir Simon's face, which was frozen in an expression of anger mixed with surprise. The wizard glanced at William with an odd smile.

"Come with me, fool. I have decided to let you stay because I need the sight of a new face to cheer me. This old crone annoys me, though I've gotten used to her company," he said, pushing Calendar out of the way. "If you please me more, I shall add her to my gallery. But if you do not please me enough, I shall add you." The wizard turned a withering glare on William, who looked away. He followed the silver-robed man back down the series of corridors, mechanically putting one foot in front of the other. With the Silver Knight imprisoned in lead once more, William was left alone to defeat the wizard. How was he ever going to do that?

A soldier showed William to a small, dark room near the gallery.

"You're to take your meals in your room. The wizard does not sleep well, so you will become used to waking at all hours."

"It's so dark down here, I think I'll lose all sense of time anyway," William said wearily. "Are you my guard?" he asked, looking more closely at the soldier. The man's mouth was almost entirely hidden by a large white mustache. His face was stern and forbidding, but the eyes that looked at William from beneath the metal helmet were kind.

"Yes." He looked as if he wanted to say more, but after a moment, he turned abruptly on his heel and left the room. The door closed, and the bolts were shot across on the other side.

William looked around his prison. The only light in the room came from two torches attached to the wall. His bed, a straw pallet on the floor, was shoved into one corner, and a rough table and stool stood in the other. He sat down on the stool and emptied the contents of his pouch on to the table. One recorder, one pair of binoculars, one stale piece of bread. That was it.

"All right, Mrs. Phillips," he whispered to the wall. "I'm in the castle. And I'm all alone."

With his head in his hands, he closed his eyes and tried to imagine her, sitting in her chamber in the castle, poking the needle in and out of the canvas, standing up to stir the fire. If he did not succeed here, she would wait for him from one day to the next, until all her food had run out, until she was too tired to walk to the gatehouse tower to watch for him, until . . . He shook his head to drive away his worst thoughts. At last, he put everything back in the pouch and, using it for a pillow, he went to sleep.

CHAPTER 15

In the next few days, William realized that the wizard was more eager for an audience than for a fool. The old man seemed to relish the hours when he could trap William and tell him tales of the particularly evil spells he'd cast, of the bad children he'd turned into toads, and the young women he'd changed into crones. When the wizard told him about the apple-tree man, William smiled to himself, knowing Dick had been freed.

But Alastor did seem amused by William's tumbling. He wanted to know the names of all the tricks, and for the next few days, he spent long hours putting William through various strings of exercises.

"Now do a round-off, a whip-back, and a back handspring," he would say.

If William objected because he was too tired or if

he could not force his body into the gyrations Alastor required, the wizard would go into a rage, shrieking at his fool.

"I control you. You must do as I say, Muggins. Do not cross me or I shall put you in the gallery," Alastor would scream.

He was a tougher taskmaster than either Robert or Mrs. Phillips. William knew if he ever got home, he would be in perfect shape for his meet.

William's guard, whose name was Brian, understood after a few days that his prisoner had no wish to escape from the castle, so he allowed him to roam more freely about the place.

"Keep out of Alastor's way," Brian warned. "And the old crone too. The wizard has sucked out her heart and replaced it with a stone. The only thing that can be said for her is that she hates him too. You can see it in her eyes when she watches him."

"Why don't you band together to overpower him?" William asked.

"He divides us so that each is rewarded if he carries tales of another. And all of us are afraid that we shall end up in the gallery. Now that the Silver Knight has been captured again, we have no hope left."

William decided to say no more.

One morning about a week after William had arrived, he was summoned to the wizard's chambers. A young man stood in front of the wizard's throne, his hands bound in front of him.

"Ah, my fool has come," Alastor announced, his shoulder jerking faster than usual. "Now we can begin. Muggins, this man was found cutting down a tree for firewood. The summer is over and the wind is blowing up out of the northwest. This man says his children are cold, but cutting down trees is against the law, is it not?"

The man spat to one side. "That is what I think of this wizard's laws," he muttered. "The wizard would have us starve and freeze. Soon there will be no person left in this godforsaken kingdom to follow his laws."

"*Silence!*" Alastor screamed, rising from his chair. "How dare you speak, you churlish scoundrel." He snatched the necklace from under his robes and pointed something at the man. As William watched, the man began to turn to lead. He screamed and clawed at his legs.

"Stop it," William cried, reaching out to take the man's hands.

He was pulled back by Brian. "Don't touch him or you'll be next," the soldier whispered in his ear.

"There, Muggins," the wizard spat when the man fell to the floor, a twisted metal statue. "A little demonstration for your further education. Now get away from me, all of you. Your faces sicken me."

The room was emptied in seconds. "I hate him," William said to Brian as they took the dark corridor back down to his room.

"Hate has no magic in it," Brian muttered. "We need magic to defeat him."

"Have you seen him do that before?"

The man nodded. Through the holes in his helmet, William could see the tears standing in the old soldier's eyes. "Too many times to count. Other people's agonies are the only pleasure Alastor takes from life."

When the wizard didn't need him, William spent long hours pacing the corridors, trying to devise a plan. He knew he had to get the necklace from around Alastor's neck, but he could not think how. He found himself drawn to the gallery of lead people again and again. He went always to stand in front of the Silver Knight and stare into his eyes, as if they held the secret to the wizard's defeat.

"What did you do?" he asked one afternoon. "March up to the castle waving your broad sword? What made you think evil like that could be struck down with an ordinary weapon?"

"Sir Simon's subjects gave him away," said a voice beside William. He turned, and to his horror he saw that Calendar had slunk up behind him. "The old wizard has spies everywhere who are so scared of him that they do whatever he tells them."

William listened to her raspy whisper without moving. The old woman knew now that he was acquainted with the Silver Knight. Would she tell Alastor? She began to speak again in such a low voice that he had to lean closer to hear her.

"When Alastor heard the Silver Knight was coming up the main road, he went out to meet him. Before Simon could lift his sword, the wizard pulled out the lead disk and froze him." She covered her eyes. "I had to watch it happening to him for a second time. Then he took the boy too. The people stood on the side of the road, their faces all twisted in despair." Suddenly her voice changed. "They are fools all of them. There is only one way to defeat Alastor."

William still didn't speak. He willed her to go on.

"But why should I tell you my secrets?" she asked. "Why shouldn't I save them for myself? Then the revenge shall be all mine."

William took a chance. "Because this is your grandson, Calendar," he whispered, nodding his head at the lead boy. "This is your daughter's son."

Her head swiveled back to the boy, and she stared into his blank, gray eyes. "The baby boy, the sickly one," she cried.

William grabbed her by the arms. "What is the secret? How do I defeat Alastor?"

Her silence seemed to last forever. In the distance, they could hear the clank of an approaching guard. The wizard was coming.

"It's the necklace first," she muttered. "Get the necklace from him, and then all you have to face is the mirror. But nobody has ever defeated the mirror."

"The mirror?" he asked in a hurried whisper. "What is the mirror?"

"It looks right through you," she said, talking more to herself now. "Shows you all the horrors inside yourself. No way to hide from the mirror. Not even Alastor could hide from that. Or you."

William sprang away from her as the large double doors were pushed open. Out of the corner of his eye, he could see Calendar roll over to crouch in her usual position in the corner.

The wizard gave them an odd look when he entered the room. "I see you both are enjoying my little gallery," he said with a chuckle. "I am usually the only one who likes to be in here. Perhaps we are three of a kind."

William shuddered at the thought and turned abruptly away. "I must go," he said.

"No," the wizard said sharply. "You will stay here. Remember, you are my fool. And not a very good one at that," he grumbled. "Guard, bring me a chair. I want my fool to give a performance for all these assembled." He swept his hand around the room to indicate the motionless audience. "Go," he shouted at the guard, who was not moving fast enough.

William didn't bother to object. In the short time he'd lived in the grim bowels of the castle, he'd grown used to the whims of the wizard. Besides, he rather liked the idea of giving a performance in front of the Silver Knight. It seemed a fitting memorial to the bravery of his old friend, useless though it had been.

The chair was brought. William took some time at the opposite end of the room, warming up and stretching out his muscles. He had a feeling this was going to be a real performance, the last important meet of the season.

"Get on with it, fool," the wizard called from his throne.

William walked to the center of the room. He bowed first to the wizard and then to the leaden audience along the walls. He felt their eyes and a curious tension began to build in him.

"Two round-offs, two back handsprings, and a cart-wheel," the wizard barked.

William nodded even though he had no intention of following the wizard's orders. He had gauged the distance. He knew the routine he would use to cross the room. And when he ended with the Arabian front somersault, he knew where his feet would land. He started with a series of cartwheels that took him around the room in a whirling circle. From his first position in the corner, he hurtled toward the wizard with two round-offs. Coming out of the second one, he punched up high in the air for the line of back handsprings that brought him closer and closer to the silver robes. As the room turned upside down over and over, William saw the wizard reaching for his necklace. The old man jumped to his feet.

"Obey me, fool," he screamed. "The Arabian."

William twisted into the Arabian and ducked his head down to end in Mrs. Phillips's special, the front somersault. As he came up, his feet caught the wizard full in the chest and knocked him to the ground.

William fell beside the wizard, shaken for a moment. It was the old crone's voice that brought him to his senses.

"*The necklace!*" she screamed. He reached across the heaving silver chest and snatched it from the wizard's neck.

A cry of pain and anger filled the room. William leaped to his feet and backed away from the curled silver figure on the floor. The wizard rose slowly. "Close the doors," he ordered the guard in a steely voice, and the man jumped to obey. With the click of the lock, there was complete silence in the room.

"I am the boy in the legend, Alastor," William

gasped, his chest still heaving. "I have come to take back the Silver Knight's kingdom."

Then a low, horrible cackle bubbled up from deep inside the wizard's throat.

"And now, fool, you think you have me. But you don't know about the mirror, do you?" Both hands were thrust inside the pockets of his billowing robe, searching for something, as he advanced on William. The wizard had grown even larger and more menacing with the loss of his necklace, and William continued to back away until he felt the solid form of the Silver Knight behind him.

"Nobody escapes the mirror. When you look inside it, you will see all the cowardice and hatred and greed inside yourself. Won't he, Calendar?" he called out to the old woman without taking his eyes off William. Her only reply was a moan of terror. "Calendar has seen the mirror do its work. Beggars and priests and kings have fallen in front of the mirror. What will it show you, fool? What are you but just a small, stupid, terrified boy?" the wizard shrieked as he pulled something out of his right-hand pocket and thrust it toward William.

William shut his eyes. He couldn't bear to have his journey end this way, after everything he'd come through.

"Open your eyes, fool. You will have to see it.

There is no resisting it," the wizard crowed, certain of his victory.

William thought once more of Mrs. Phillips, the one person who believed in him. *You have inside you the heart and soul of a knight,* she had said.

He opened his eyes and looked into the mirror. All he saw was the figure of himself, William, walking slowly but surely toward him. As the figure got closer, he could see the picture of Mrs. Phillips imprisoned inside his heart.

"What does he see, Calendar?" the wizard cried.

"He sees himself, Alastor. And the lady he has taken prisoner. Nothing else."

"But I'm here so that lady can go free," William said, his voice powerful in the silent room. He took another step toward the mirror. It no longer scared him. It showed him only what he already knew. With every forward stride that William made, the wizard retreated until he was trapped in a corner of the room, his eyes wide, his mouth open and waiting for a scream that never came. William reached out and snatched the mirror, turning it on Alastor.

The look of horror on the wizard's face was unbearable, and William was almost tempted to drop the mirror and break it.

Alastor sank to his knees, covering his eyes with his hands. "It's the locust," he moaned.

"The destroyer, the ravager," Calendar shrieked, her arms lifted up to the ceiling. Hatred was etched in every line on her face. Before William could stop her, Calendar had snatched the necklace that dangled from his left hand. She pointed the lead disk at the wizard and mumbled the word "Saturn." Alastor reached up and tried to grab the length of ribbon from her, but she swung it back and forth just above his grasp. His legs had already turned to lead from the feet to the knees, and he began to drag himself about the floor on his elbows, trying to catch her. He looked like a wounded animal.

"Calendar, no," William shouted. "Stop it. We can take care of him some other way. Don't do that to him."

But she was lost to anything but her own revenge. Dancing around the twisted, gray form of the wizard, she flipped the lead disk and muttered another word William couldn't hear. Alastor was gone.

Before anybody could stop him, William raised his arms and smashed the mirror to the floor. It shattered instantly into a hundred scattered slivers.

CHAPTER 16

William stepped across the place where the wizard had twisted in his last agonies and took the necklace from Calendar's hands. She gave it up without a word and sank to the floor, sobbing, crouched in her familiar position.

He glanced up at the soldiers still standing at attention by the door. They were staring at him speechlessly.

"I have no wish to fight you," he said.

Brian, his guard, was the first to react. "My lord," he said, with a formal bow. "We thank you for our freedom from the wizard's tyranny. We are at your command."

"Not mine, Brian, but this man's," William said, going over to stand in front of Sir Simon. "But how do we break the lead spell? How can we bring him back to life?"

Brian went to Calendar and muttered something in her ear, but she just shook her head and pushed him away.

"She will not tell me how to undo the spell, my lord," he said.

"I don't think she knows how," William said. "I guess the wizard never undid any of his spells. But I have an idea. I have brought Sir Simon back to life once. Maybe I can do it again."

While the soldiers watched, William put his arms around his old friend and pressed his cheek against the cold metal wrinkles of his tunic. "Come back, Sir Simon," he whispered. "Your kingdom has been retaken." Suddenly, William felt those arms crushing him in a familiar hug, and he looked up to see the knight's eyes filled with tears.

"Sir Simon," he cried. "You are alive."

The knight didn't speak but held his squire at arm's length as if to study his face more closely. Then he looked slowly around the room.

"The wizard?" he asked.

"He is gone. We have defeated him."

"Your weapons were stronger than mine, William."

William looked away, embarrassed. "I see you found

yourself a page," he said, taking the lead hands of Dick's son into his own. Gradually, they warmed and turned to flesh. The boy's eyes lost their blank gaze and focused on William.

"You did as I asked and brought the Silver Knight to me," William said gently. The boy nodded. "What's your name?"

"Tolliver, if you please, sir."

William smiled. "You weren't calling me sir before, Tolliver."

"No," the boy replied with a grin.

"What about the others?" Sir Simon asked. "How do we bring them back?"

"I think I can do it," William said. "It seems to work the same way it did in the castle." He went from one lead figure to another, touching a cheek here, a hand there, until the room was filled with live people, asking questions and stretching their stiff limbs. As the story of the wizard's defeat was passed from one to another, they pressed forward to shake William's hand.

When that was done, he took Tolliver and Sir Simon over to the corner where Calendar still crouched. He touched her on the shoulder.

"Calendar," he said softly, "I've brought some people to see you. Here is Sir Simon and Tolliver, your grandson."

She would not look up but pulled William down beside her. "I cannot bear to have them see me like this, a wizened old lady with a black heart. You never knew me to be any different, but Simon was my beloved one before the days of the wizard."

Sir Simon took her hands and lifted her up so that he could see her face. Then he hugged her. "My beloved old Calendar."

That hug of Sir Simon's and the love in his voice melted Calendar as quickly as William's hands had softened the leaden bodies. For the first time since William had met her, he saw her smile.

"You do not hate me, my lord," she cried. "I should have struggled harder with Alastor to rescue you."

"Even if you had, there was nothing you could do against his power. These years with the wizard must have been very lonely ones." She closed her eyes as if to shut out the horrible memories. "But the wizard's spells are broken, thanks to our good friend, William," Sir Simon went on. "You will stay with me and live out your life in comfort, surrounded by your friends."

"And your family," William cried, pushing Tolliver forward. The old woman and the young boy stared at each other, then joined hands, then hugged. William thought he'd never seen two people look so happy, and he felt the tears coming into his own eyes. For once, he let them slide down his cheeks, and when Calendar caught sight of them, she reached up to brush them away.

"It's all right, Calendar. I'm just so happy for you."

"I know, my gentle lord. I know you are."

At a signal from Sir Simon, Tolliver led his grandmother off to a corner of the room, where they sat down immediately and began to talk.

"Now you must put the necklace on," Sir Simon said. "It holds the token you will need for the Lady Elinore."

William looked more closely at the prize he'd come such a long way to get. Two medallions dangled from the long red ribbon. The first was the reverse side of the Janus medal that Mrs. Phillips held back in the castle. It looked identical except for a kinder expression on the god's face and the two keys engraved on either side of his head.

"The keys to her freedom," he said, showing the token to Sir Simon.

"And this is the lead disk," the knight said.

"What are those markings on the top?" William asked.

Sir Simon picked up the medal rather gingerly and peered at it. "That's the sign of Saturn," he said. "According to the old alchemists, lead was associated with Saturn, the god of death and decay. An evil sign."

William slipped the lead medal off the ribbon. "I only need the Janus token," he said. "You take this and keep it somewhere safe. I don't want it to fall into the wrong hands."

There was no time for further discussion, as the crowds were pressing forward once more.

Brian appeared by William's side with a big black cat in his arms.

"Where did that come from?" William asked.

"The spells are all broken," Brian explained. "This is Calendar's cat. You knew him better as the dragon that guarded the castle gates."

William looked into the animal's eyes, but he saw no horrible pictures of fire, only a calm, mysterious expression. Suddenly, the cat meowed.

"I think he's hungry, sir," Brian said. "I shall see that he gets something to eat."

William was eager to return home immediately, but the Silver Knight insisted that a celebration be held first, so a huge banquet was prepared. In the baronial hall upstairs, William sat at the high table between Sir Simon and Dick, the apple-tree man, who had come to the castle looking for his son. Each plate was heaped with good things, and each cup was full to the brim. While they waited for all to be seated, William asked

Sir Simon something he'd been wanting to know.

"How did you get out of the forest, Sir Simon? I stood and called your name, hoping my voice would lead you back to me."

Sir Simon shook his head, staring down at his plateful of meats, breads, and savories. "To think that I should be fooled by the vision of Moonlight. But Lord Luck himself must have been walking beside me because eventually, after much wandering and at the edge of despair, I found myself next to a real stream. I followed it out of the forest, knowing that at least I was going in one direction and not in endless circles." He turned to Dick, the apple-tree man. "Tolliver found me and told me that William had gone ahead. I made such haste to catch up with him that I must have passed him altogether."

"I'm afraid he was up a tree for a very long time, thanks to me," Dick replied, smiling at William.

"Well, we are all together now, and that's what counts," said Sir Simon. Standing up, he knocked on the table with his fist until the great hall fell silent. Then he raised his tankard. "Here's to young William, who found his own way through the dark forest. He alone has defeated the curse of a man who held our kingdom prisoner for far too long. Let each of us remember the lesson William has taught us. The weapons that you need to fight the battle are inside your own heart. To William," he shouted. "To William," answered a hundred happy voices.

William jumped to his feet and put up his hands for silence. When the tumult had subsided, he raised his own tankard and shouted, "To the Lady Elinore."

"To the Lady Elinore," they roared back. They drank deeply, one and all, and the eating began, to the sound of laughter, music, and the cheerful thunk of the wooden bowls against the trestle tables.

"What is all this food?" William asked as one serving plate after another was carried into the banquet hall.

"Boar's head with pudding, squirrel stew, boiled chickens, cakes with sliced apples," Dick rattled off, pointing to the various piles on William's plate.

"But where did it all come from? The land I traveled through could not possibly have produced this much food."

"The moment the wizard was defeated, the land sprang back to life as if there had never been a famine," Dick explained.

After filling his stomach, William gave up all effort at conversation and sat back to enjoy the scene. The good food and the hot, sweet cider lulled him to sleep, and later on in the evening, he felt Sir Simon's strong arms carrying him to bed.

* * *

When William woke the next morning, Tolliver was waiting for him with a basin of water.

"What will you do now that the wizard has gone?" William asked, splashing his face.

"Sir Simon says I may stay in the castle and be apprenticed to one of the squires. I asked if it could be you, sir, but he told me you are leaving us. I wish you would stay."

"There is someone waiting for me at home." The thought of Mrs. Phillips made him more eager than ever to be on his way.

William ate a quick breakfast with Sir Simon, who was quiet after the revelry of the night before. "Will it be just as difficult to get through the forest going the other way, Sir Simon?" William asked.

"You've forgotten, William, that the spells are broken. The forest is harmless now. Tolliver wishes to go with you. I shall give you each a horse, and he can lead yours back when he has seen you safely to your castle gates. There will be enough food in the packs so that you can take some back to the Lady Elinore. I expect she has finished off all the mice in the attic by now."

"Thank you." William slid his chair back, but Sir Simon's voice stopped him. "Please send my kindest regards to her. I shall miss her . . ." His voice drifted off. He shook himself and stood up. "I doubt we shall meet again, young William," he said as they embraced. "But we shall live in each other's thoughts forever."

William held on to his old friend for an extra moment. "I can't believe you won't be waiting for me in the attic after school," he whispered. For the second time in as many days, William began to cry, but he didn't try to hold back his tears. It was right to feel sad. It was right to show it. "Goodbye, Sir Simon," he said. "I'll never forget you."

William and Tolliver rode out into the cool morning. When the steep hill leading away from the castle dipped down the first time, William turned to look back. The black pennant had been replaced with a silver flag, which curled lazily in the early morning breeze. Sir Simon stood on the wall walk next to one of his guards, his arm raised in farewell. William returned the wave and pressed his horse forward with a sharp kick.

The return journey took two days. Tolliver was an easy companion, respectful of William's silence but eager to serve him whenever possible.

Everyone they passed greeted them cheerfully, and often people pressed food on them or directed them to the nearest source of water for a cool drink. The news of the wizard's defeat had given the people renewed hope, and they had returned to reclaim their land.

William and Tolliver spent the night at the edge of the forest, and in the morning, William handed his horse over to the page.

"I go alone from here, Tolliver. Take your master's horse back to him with all my best wishes for his continued good health and happiness."

"But sir, I was to go all the way with you," Tolliver said.

"I want to spend this last day alone," William explained.

"Goodbye, then. We won't forget you," Tolliver said. "Good luck to you."

"And to you," William replied as he turned away from the wistful face and was lost in the dark coolness of the forest.

This time there were no tempting visions, no noisy roar of angry animals. A cool path patterned by spots of sunlight led through the trees. Every now and then, an animal rustled away at the sound of William's footsteps. When he stopped, he could hear the high, clean notes of birds singing to one another in the thick branches.

It took an afternoon to walk from the far edge of the forest to the castle. William reached the gates just as the sun was setting. Before he had time to raise his hand or shout a greeting, he heard the familiar creak of the windlass as the portcullis was raised and the wooden doors were opened. Then, ever so slowly, the drawbridge was lowered. He jumped the last foot of space before it hit the ground. Mrs. Phillips was waiting for him under the front archway.

CHAPTER 17

"My warrior has returned," Mrs. Phillips said, holding him at arm's length.

"Do I look any different?" asked William.

"Perhaps a little wiser," she said, cocking her head to one side. "But otherwise no different."

"But don't I look taller and stronger now that I have defeated the wizard?" He flexed the muscles in his right arm.

"Nonsense. You were always strong enough. You just didn't believe it."

They ate dinner together in the courtyard the way they had during the week of training. The table seemed larger and less welcoming without the knight.

"Sir Simon sent you his best wishes," William told her.

"He's a good man with a big heart, but he lacks

imagination. My dear husband, Alfred, was the same way. He would attack one problem over and over again like a baby butting its head against the side of its crib. But that's neither here nor there. I want you to tell me about your adventures."

"Didn't the tapestry show you?" William asked.

"Yes. I know the bare outlines. Now I want to hear the details."

William told her the whole story, dragging out the scary parts and glossing over the moments when he'd made a mistake or his courage had failed him. When he was done, she sat back in her chair as if she'd just finished an enormous meal.

"Now you know the answer to all your own questions, William. A truly courageous person is the one who must first conquer fear within himself." She stood up. "Come with me to view your booty."

"What do you mean, my booty?" he asked as he followed her up the tower stairs. When she pushed open her bedroom door, he could see nothing different about the room. He stepped forward to examine the tapestry that stood in front of the fireplace, but her voice stopped him.

"Not that, William. Over in the corner behind you."

He turned around, vaguely aware of a dark shape over his right shoulder. He had taken two more steps across the room before he realized what he was looking at. "It's the wizard," he cried. "In lead. So this is where Calendar sent him."

"A few days ago, he appeared in my room out of nowhere. I looked up from my stitching and there he was. I knew from the tapestry that you'd triumphed, but I didn't expect such an unwelcome visitor."

William walked up and looked more closely at his old enemy's face. It was frozen in the look of horror that the mirror had produced, the creases around his lips and eyes curled into gray metal, the mouth open in an anguished cry.

"He saw a locust in the mirror. It must have been horrible," William said in a voice filled with awe. "I'm glad I broke the mirror. Nobody should have the power to look at the secrets inside another person." He reached up to touch the wizard's cheek.

"Don't, William!" Mrs. Phillips cried. "Remember what your touch will do."

He drew his hand back just in time. "I forgot," he said, his voice shaky.

Mrs. Phillips took his arm and led him gently away.

They decided to spend one more night in the castle. The two of them secured the drawbridge and took a last stroll around the wall walk.

"I'm not quite ready to go back," William said.

"I know what you mean," Mrs. Phillips said. "The world out there doesn't seem quite as important anymore, although I shall be glad to get a new jar of Marmite and take a brisk walk in the countryside instead of around and around the courtyard."

"I had forgotten you've been cooped up in here a pretty long time."

She stopped and looked at him. "Now, when I head down that path to the bus stop tomorrow afternoon, William, no funny business, right?"

"Right," he said. "Although I do have this special token that makes people green from the roots of their hair right down to their toenails. Don't you think your brother would like you to come home a whole new color?" He dodged away from the punch that she aimed at his shoulder.

The next morning they ate the last of the granola for breakfast and changed into their old clothes. They met downstairs in the courtyard and raised the portcullis together.

"You get the wooden doors, William," said Mrs. Phillips. She was carrying her suitcase, the old blue raincoat, and the fire screen. She saw William looking at it.

"I know it will be clumsy, but I want a record of our adventures," she said a bit sheepishly. "Have you got everything? Where's Bear?"

"In my backpack. I wouldn't leave him behind no matter what," William said.

"Where shall we do it?"

"Just outside the castle, so we don't damage anything when we grow. If we stood on the drawbridge, we'd break it."

"You're right. I've gotten awfully used to myself this size," she said.

"Sure you don't want to stay this way?" he asked.

"Yes, young William, I am very sure," she replied with just a hint of Sir Simon in her voice. "Now, lower the drawbridge, my lord. We have business to attend to outside the castle."

"As you wish, my lady."

Arm in arm, they walked over the wooden planks for the last time. "Look back," she said. "It will never look this way again." William remembered the time he'd seen the castle when the Silver Knight first made him small. Every detail of the stonework and every line in the planking had suddenly stood out.

After a moment, she pulled open the leather pouch and he produced the necklace.

"Does it need to be back together?" she asked.

"I don't know," he said. "Let's try it that way first."

They pressed the two halves of the token together and snapped the clasps on either side.

"I'll do you first," he said. "It's only fair."

Before she could object, he pointed the key side of the token at her and said the word "Janus." Suddenly he was looking at the pattern of holes in the toes of her comfortable brown shoes. She knelt down and picked him up very carefully.

"Now I know how you felt," he called out to her.

"I'm putting you down on the top stair where I can point it at you," she said quietly. "Put the token in the palm of my hand."

He dropped it carefully. He felt himself being lifted up again. It was an eerie sensation that reminded him of going up in an elevator, except this one had no sides. He glanced down at Mrs. Phillips's palm.

"You have an enormous life line," he called, and she smiled.

"Crawl off now, but be careful you don't tumble over the edge."

William stationed himself in the middle of the top step and waited. She was leaning over the castle.

"What are you doing?" he called.

She put the roof back down on top of the bedchambers. "Getting the wizard," she replied as she slipped the lead figure into her pocket. "It's not safe to leave him here with you. You might forget one day and pick him up."

"Why don't you just put me in the other pocket and

take me to England with you?" he said.

"Oh, William, don't tempt me," she said. Her voice sounded gruff. "Are you ready to grow?"

He nodded. As she pointed, holding the token in between her thumb and her index finger, he closed his eyes again. Except for the slight sensation of air passing his face, he felt nothing.

"Open your eyes, William," she said, and he knew the magic had worked for the last time.

Downstairs, the clock was striking four-fifteen. They stopped for a moment in the kitchen so that she could look around.

"Just when I left," he said, nodding at the calendar by the refrigerator. "You know how careful Mom is about crossing off the days." He glanced at her. "I'm sorry about the time you lost."

"It makes me feel younger," she said with a smile. "We'd better go. The bus should be coming soon."

He took her suitcase, and they walked out the same path they had taken before.

"Do you still have the token?" he asked.

"Yes. The wizard's in one pocket and the token's in the other. I'll drop them both off the side of the ship when I cross the Atlantic."

"Want to see my floor routine for the meet? I could

do it right here on the grass," he said. "We have time before the bus comes."

"Robert wouldn't approve. The ground is so uneven."

"Never mind, we won't tell him," William said.

"All right," she said. "Do the one you used to knock over Alastor."

So right there on the grass, he did a round-off, two back handsprings, with an Arabian front somersault.

"No spotting," she cried as she burst into applause. "That's all I ever was. Your spotter."

He ran to her, and she put her arms around him one last time. "Goodbye," he said into her rumpled dress. They both could hear the roar of the bus's engines as it started up the last hill toward them. He hung on until the last minute, but in the end he was the first to take his arms away. She picked up her suitcase and climbed the bus steps without looking back. Long after the door had closed and the bus had grumbled away from the stop, he stood on the side of the road and waved.

When he went back into the kitchen to pour himself a bowl of cereal, he noticed the note taped under the telephone. "William, Chicken with cashew nuts tonight. I'll do the shopping. Love, Dad."

AUTHOR'S NOTE

*Every piece of writing ... starts from what I call
a grit ... a sight or sound, a sentence or a happening that does not pass away ... but quite in-
explicably lodges in the mind.*

RUMER GODDEN

This book, my first flight into fantasy, would never have
left the ground without the support of many friends.

First, thanks to Jan Perkins, who introduced me to the
work of Joseph Campbell. His lecture on Parsifal and the
Holy Grail was the first "grit."

Thanks to Margery Cuyler, my tireless editor, who prod-
ded me to get my feet off the ground, to take the flight.
Soon after her exhortation, I had a dream that I was standing
in a room in my bare feet. Margery was standing next to
me. I left the room, and when I came back she had planted
bulbs in my shoes. "Margery," I said, "how am I supposed
to walk?" "Don't think about walking," she said. "Think
about the flowers."

Thanks to writing friends who sympathize, listen, criti-
cize, and rejoice—Alison Herzig, Margaret Robinson, Betsy
Sachs, Anne Crile, Jenny Lawrence, Sarah Meredith, Vir-
ginia Carry, and Barbara Shikler.

Thanks to Eleanor Miller. She took over for me so that I could write, she gave us the castle, and she knew when the time had come to leave.

Thanks to Rudy Van Daele of the Life Sport Gymnastics Program in New York City and to Roberto Pumpido, coach of the West Side Y team, for their input both as coaches and as gymnasts. And to Liza Burnett, who helped me understand what it feels like.

And thanks above all to my family.

Now I understand what Katherine Paterson meant when she said, "The very persons who have taken away my time and space are those who have given me something to say."

—Elizabeth Winthrop
January, 1985

About the Author

ELIZABETH WINTHROP is the author of more than twenty books for children of all ages. She has lectured on writing in schools and colleges around the country. Ms. Winthrop is married to Peter Mahony, an architect, and they live with their two children in New York City.